THE GIRL WHO DIGS GRAVES

BOOK ONE OF THE GRAVEDIGGERS SERIES

THE GIRL WHO DIGS GRAVES

WILLIE E. DALTON

To my Daddy,

This isn't one my books I would have wanted to you
to read, but I know you would have been proud of me
just the same. I miss you more every single day.

PROLOGUE

THE SCENT OF FRESHLY TURNED EARTH FILLED her nostrils. The air was warm on her skin, but not thick or heavy with humidity. It could be hard digging graves on hot nights, though not as hard as it was in the winter. The thought of working in winter made her shiver: icy air burning her throat and lungs; sweat running down her back under all the layers of clothes, while she chipped away at the frozen earth.

But tonight was a good night; the air was nice and she could observe the lightning bugs flitting about. The dirt turned easily beneath her shovel. The job would go by fast. There was no big tangle of roots to cut or fight, and the rocks she dug up were handled by the shovel alone. If only every night was this easy.

"How's it going, girl?" A deep, ragged, voice cut through the darkness.

"Another hour and it should be done," she said, and kept shoveling. The light from her lantern showed her the progress she was making on the grave, but she couldn't see anything outside of the pit.

"You're moving fast tonight," the old man's voice replied.

"It's been an easy one," she grunted as she tossed out another shovel full of dirt.

"Here, let me work on it a while," the old man said as he clambered down into the hole with her.

"I don't mind to do it; I know you haven't been feeling your best." She looked at him, watching for signs of pain or fatigue.

"Nah, I'm ok right now. It's been a while since I worked on one," he said, taking the shovel from her.

She relinquished the shovel and climbed up on the edge of the grave. She watched him dig. Even at his age and in ill health, he still dug much faster than she did—something only decades of experience could teach, she supposed.

Her eyes wandered around the quiet graveyard; normal people would be uncomfortable out here this late—well, except for a few wannabe-devil-worshipers, who always looked silly. Then there were the hoodoo and voodoo practitioners who stopped by to get graveyard dirt for their magical workings; they were usually nice, and respectful of the dead.

She'd lived in this graveyard pretty much her whole life. She had been born from her mother's death. A brutal car accident had killed her mother a few weeks before she was due to give birth. The first person on the scene had been a former E.R. physician, who just happened to hear the crash. He called for an ambulance, but knew there was no time to wait to get the baby out, since the mother was already deceased. He'd cut her mom open on the roadside and saved the baby's life: her life.

Her dad had been so grief-stricken that he'd shot himself in front of his wife's grave, with no thought to the baby beside him.

The cemetery caretaker, who was also the local

gravedigger, had taken in the baby to raise, and dug a grave for her dad next to her mom.

It was a good life, although most people didn't understand it. He was good to her: he'd sent her to school, taught her his trade when she'd showed an interest; and above all, he'd loved her. He told her stories of how he'd worked with her when she was a baby: sometimes he'd let one of the local church women babysit while he dug, other times he'd swaddled her up and let her sleep on a blanket while he attended to his duties.

When she was old enough to realize grave digging wasn't the most normal job in the world, she'd asked him about it.

He'd told her he hadn't always been a gravedigger. In his younger years, he was a doctor—an E.R. doctor, to be exact.

He'd spent many years saving and losing lives, counting each loss as a failure on his part—until the day he realized: not everyone could, or even should, be saved.

Some people were so far gone or broken by the time they came to him that it would require machines to keep them alive, and even then, it would only serve to prolong their remaining days. They had to take enough pills to fill a bathtub to keep their hearts pumping and make their pain bearable, then take more pills on top of those to keep the others from killing them.

True, for some, anything was better than death. Even though they were keeping death at bay with the fire of a dimming torch, it was better than surrendering to the unknown.

Others wanted to die, and they told him so; they

cried and yelled at him for saving them, for stringing out their suffering, either mental or physical. And in a lot of situations he understood their frustration; he learned quickly in his career that there were fates far worse than death.

He had wanted away from all of it, but hadn't found his new calling until he treated the town's cemetery keeper. He thought being around death all the time would be too sad. But the little old gravedigger just seemed peaceful. So, he asked him his secret.

The cemetery keeper told him, "Dealing with the dead is easy. You dig their grave, bury them, pay your respects, and watch over their final resting place. It's where we all end up on this earth." He followed it up with, "Being around so much death, you can see it in people when their time is close, even if they don't realize it yet. But I realize it, and I'm leaving soon."

It turned out the old man was right: he was soon diagnosed with pancreatic cancer. Before he died, he took on the doctor as an apprentice, and taught him everything he knew to continue as the cemetery keeper in his place. He gave him his cabin on the grounds to live in, and all the tools he would need.

The doctor had lived there by himself a few years, then one night he'd heard a gunshot. He'd found the body of a dead man across the grave of a woman he had recently buried. Next to the man's grizzly corpse was a screaming baby that had been left in her car seat. The man recognized the baby as the one he delivered on the roadside only a week before.

Being a well-respected man in town, and knowing all the right people, had worked out to his advantage. The adoption had gone through quickly, and from the first night, that little girl was his.

She had heard all the stories and walked by her parent's graves every day, though she couldn't say she felt a lot when she saw those aging headstones. The gravedigger (or Ray, as she called him) had been her dad. Even watching other kids at school with their parents, she didn't feel like she was missing out. She wasn't envious of their fights with their moms, or of the awkward conversations with their dads. Ray never grounded her, but then again, she never asked to do anything.

She liked being at the cemetery with him. The smell of the grass and tending to the stones and flowers made her happy. Digging the graves made her happy.

She watched Ray dig for a while until she could hear his labored breathing.

"Here, let me finish it," she said, jumping back down into the hole. "Who is this one for?" she asked him. It always felt a little funny when it was for someone she knew or saw often, but she liked to know just the same.

Ray leaned against the dirt and eyed her as he used his handkerchief to wipe away the sweat from his head and neck. She was strong and capable; he had done a good job with her—as well as anyone could have, he thought.

She stopped digging and turned to face him, waiting for his response.

"It's mine, Hel."

She stared at him. While part of her mind searched for words, the other part scanned her body for emotion. Nothing. No words, no feelings, just a hollow emptiness.

She started digging again.

CHAPTER ONE

It was just a few months past my twenty-second birthday when Ray died. Lucky for me, the mayor and important people in town honored his will and let me keep my job and cabin. After all, they knew I could do the work.

Death doesn't stop for grief. I dug at least six more graves right after I lost Ray, and had barely slowed down since.

Being busy doesn't bother me, and my routine didn't change that much—even though it's just me now.

I go into town once a week for groceries and new library books. Everyone tries to be nice to me, and most people know who I am; but I'm still the weird girl in town, even though they've known me for years.

It's a typical small Appalachian town. You knew where it was because you grew up in it or near it; otherwise people only found it by getting lost trying to go somewhere else.

I missed Ray, but I hadn't mourned him—at least, not in the way most people mourn. I didn't cry or get angry. I did miss having him to talk to, so I talked to myself. Maybe one day, I'd get a dog or something.

It wasn't uncommon for my phone to ring late at night or early in the morning with someone telling me about an upcoming funeral. I generally had about three to five days from the time of the call to get the grave dug.

Certain times were busier than others, though, like holidays; people always seemed to die more around holidays. That could make it hard to keep everything on schedule. Sometimes it took Ray and I both working on separate graves throughout the night to get it done. That could pose a challenge this year.

Many people asked why we didn't get modern and use heavy equipment, like most cemeteries nowadays. Ray believed every person deserves to have someone work hard for their final resting place: to have someone pour their sweat and attention into the job, knowing it was where we all end up.

Also, here in the Appalachian mountains where we live there are little hidden family cemeteries stuck way up on hillsides. Big machinery can't always get up those steep places, so when that happens, they call us as well.

This morning was no different from many others: I got up and made my coffee as usual. The cabin was quiet except for the creak of the floors under my feet. I could feel the chill of autumn creeping in through the window screens. It was just cool enough to make you reach for your robe first thing in the morning, but you knew you would sweat by noon. I resisted the urge to turn on the heat, knowing coffee would do the trick, if it ever finished percolating.

Ray, would only drink percolated coffee; he said it was the only way worth drinking it. I would drink other coffee if it was offered to me, but he was right: his way was the best.

I made my breakfast the same as most mornings: four eggs, four pieces of bacon, and a biscuit. Ray said getting plenty of protein was important in our line of work because it was so physical. I'd load up on vegetables with dinner. Every day I did the same things, wandering from chore to chore around the house, hearing Ray's voice telling me what to do and why to do it. I was grateful he had taught me how to take care of myself, and that he left me capable enough to maintain the job he trained me to do.

The phone rang.

"Caretaker," I answered.

"Hey there, Helena. How are you?" Mr. Akins asked.

"I'm good. How are you?" I didn't really care about formalities in business conversations, but I was polite just the same.

"I'm well, thank you. We need a spot for a young woman in plot sixty-five-A," he said.

"Ok, when do you need it?" I asked.

"By Thursday morning." He said the words like he was trying to spit them out. "I know that's pretty fast. Can you do it? I can have Joe come down with his backhoe."

I felt my face get hot, but allowed only confidence to come out of my mouth. "I got it, Mr. Akins."

"Great, thanks." He hung up.

They kept giving me less and less notice. Ray they had respected, because they'd known him as a doctor before he took on the job; they assumed he was eccentric from all his time in trauma. But let a young woman do the job and everyone freaks.

With a sigh, I put my long, dirty-blonde hair up on my head, washed my coffee cup and plate in the sink, and put on my jeans and boots.

I grabbed my gloves, mattock, and shovel from the porch. I knew where the space was, so I didn't bother taking my map with me.

It was still early, and the sun was hiding behind fluffy gray clouds. It looked like it could rain later. I thought how great it would be to get half the work done this morning, and the other half tonight, if the weather cooperated.

I used the mattock first to break up the earth so it would move more easily, then I used the shovel to clear what I had softened. Repeat… for hours.

The crunch of gravel under tires caused me to look toward the iron gate at the entrance of the cemetery. I saw a silver Jeep park, and a man got out. His hair was sleek, long, and black; his clothes were black, and his skin was pale. A goth, maybe?

I watched as he meandered around the cemetery. He'd occasionally stop to read a name or take a picture of a headstone. I had seen a few goth teenagers stop by here before, but he looked older, and not as dramatic. From where I was I didn't spot any eyeliner or black lipstick. Maybe he just liked wearing black.

This cemetery was old; there were tall tombstones well over a hundred years old, covered with moss and worn by time. The spiked iron fence was nearly seven feet tall, and went the full perimeter of the fifteen-acre lot. The gate itself was intricate and made a very satisfying creak when opened or closed. People had asked me to fix the noise a few times because it was "creepy," but I enjoyed the sound, so I let it stay.

The tall man finally looked my direction and saw me watching him. He stared for a moment, and then he did something I didn't expect: he raised his camera and snapped my picture.

Annoyed, I called out, "You should ask for permission before taking someone's picture." He smiled, and I realized he was quite handsome underneath all of that darkness and hair. He walked towards me.

"I'm sorry," he said, as he stepped in close and offered to shake my hand.

I held up my hands, still inside the dirty gloves, and shrugged. I saw no point in taking them off; my hands would be sweaty and gross.

"If you don't like the picture I took you can delete it," he said looking at me.

He had the bluest eyes I had ever seen.

"It's ok, I guess." I hesitated. "But why did you want a picture of me standing here in work clothes?"

"I was just fascinated when I saw you. I've stopped at a lot of graveyards, and I've never seen anyone, especially a woman, hand digging a grave. It was beautiful," he said. He eyed me, and then the grave I was digging.

I wasn't sure what he was calling beautiful, but it made me feel strangely proud.

"I'm Raphael," he said.

"I'm Helena," I replied. "Hel, for short." I knew his given name probably wasn't Raphael, more like Ralph. But I preferred to be called Hel, and most people refused, so I'd call him whatever he liked.

"Hel?" He gave a slight smile and raised an eyebrow. "You dig graves and your name is Hel?" He was grinning now.

I found I was grinning too, but I wasn't really sure why. "Yes, I prefer Hel, but most people call me Helena. Only Ray ever called me Hel."

"Who is Ray?" Raphael asked.

"He was the last caretaker; he raised me," I said.

Raphael nodded. "Where is he now?"

I walked about ten headstones down, three across, and pointed.

"I'm sorry" he said, and a look of concern passed his face. "Did you…" He paused, then started again. "Did you dig his grave?"

I looked down at Ray's headstone and smiled. "We dug it together."

"He helped dig his own grave?" he asked.

Impressively, he managed to look a little paler.

"Yep."

I walked a little farther into the cemetery. There was a big statue of a weeping angel looking down over the grave of an infant. The angel's face was nearly worn smooth by time and weather. All my life I could never decide if I liked her, or found her somewhat menacing. I named her Gabrielle when I was ten.

I stopped a few stones behind Gabby and pointed again. "These are my parents."

Raphael walked over and put his hand on my shoulder. I flinched; few people had ever touched me, and they weren't strangers like this guy.

"I am so sorry," he said.

I let him keep his hand on my shoulder. "It's nothing to be sorry about. I don't remember them."

"Do you have any other family or close friends?" he asked.

"No family that I know of from my parents, at least

none that cared. Ray had a few family members and an ex-wife, but I never had much to do with them. Friends?" I just kind of shrugged.

"Don't you get lonely?" he asked.

I smiled. "Because I don't have friends or family?"

"Yeah." He brushed his long dark hair from his face.

"Sometimes. Do you have friends and family?" I asked.

"Some," he nodded.

"Don't you still get lonely sometimes?"

He looked a little embarrassed. "Sometimes," he said.

The sun was no longer hidden behind the clouds, and it was getting hot out just standing still.

"I need to get back to work. I'd like to have at least half of this grave dug before it gets too hot." I turned from him and walked back to the plot.

"Can I help?" he asked.

His question caught me off guard. No one had ever offered to help me dig a grave before, except Ray. I thought for a moment while I scanned his face for sincerity.

"Come back tonight at eight, in work clothes." I looked back at him over my shoulder as I walked away. He was smiling.

CHAPTER TWO

THE GRAVE WAS HALF FINISHED WHEN I WENT inside to have lunch and cool off. I wondered if Raphael would really come back tonight. Part of me hoped that he would, it would be a nice change to have someone around.

After lunch I took a short nap, read a few chapters in my library book (a thriller), and made myself dinner of macaroni and cheese, baked chicken, and a big salad. I found myself watching the hours slowly tick by. At ten minutes until eight, I put my boots on and walked toward the cemetery.

As I got closer to the plot, I saw Raphael walking towards me in a tight black t-shirt, worn jeans, and black hiking boots, with his shiny black hair pulled back into a ponytail. He still looked too clean to dig a grave.

"Hey there," he grinned, walking up to me.

"Hi," I smiled.

"You didn't think I'd come back did you?" he asked.

"It was a fifty-fifty chance," I replied. "I guess you will need a shovel and some gloves."

"Do you have extras?"

"You can use Ray's stuff," I said.

"Is that OK?" he asked.

"Yes, he'd be happy his things are getting use. Follow me." I turned to walk back to the shed behind the cabin.

"Do you live here?" Raphael asked.

"I do," I said, handing him the gloves and shovel. It was nice getting them out of the shed again.

"It doesn't creep you out, living all by yourself in a graveyard?"

I laughed. "I was raised here, and I work here. You were the one out exploring a cemetery for fun."

"Hmm," he mumbled. "You might have a point."

We walked back toward our work.

"Why do you like wearing all black and hanging out in cemeteries?" I asked him.

"Well, I just like the color. And I find cemeteries peaceful: I like to think about what kinds of lives the people led, and what they're up to now."

"What they're up to now?" I laughed. "They're not up to anything, they're dead. I get the peacefulness though."

"You don't believe in the afterlife?" he asked. "You've never seen a ghost or gotten a cold chill out here? You can explain everything you've ever seen?"

I looked at him for a long moment and thought about his question. I must have stared at him too long, because he said, "If you keep thinking, we won't get any work done."

I nodded, and he helped me pull the tarp back.

"Is there a certain way to do this?" he asked, looking down at the bare earth.

I pointed to some lines I had marked in paint on the

grass.

"Stay inside those perimeters, and I'll let you know when we're deep enough."

He nodded and started digging. We didn't talk, we just worked. Once or twice I saw him watching my technique and trying to do the same. Raphael stopped long before I did to wipe away the sweat dripping down his face and get a drink of water.

"You do this every day?" he asked, as he took off his shirt and wiped his face.

"Pretty much, since I was about eleven or twelve." I watched him for a moment. He was in decent shape, but I could tell it was gym work, not manual labor. It was nice to look at all the same.

I nodded to his shirt in his hand. "No fair, I can't do that."

"Who says? It's just us, and it's dark out here," he smiled.

I knew he was flirting, but I had on a sports bra, so I wouldn't exactly be indecent. Raphael didn't do a great job of hiding his surprise when I stripped off my own t-shirt and tossed it up on the side of the grave. He recovered well though.

He stared at me. "I don't mean to be a creep, but you have a really great figure."

I felt my cheeks burn at the compliment. "Um, thanks."

"Don't you realize that?" he asked.

"No, I don't suppose so. I mean, I'm not pretty in the traditional, girly way. I'm quite muscular, and I don't really have any curves." I looked down at my arms and stomach. True, I was thin, but I always thought I had a boy's body type: straight hips, and lean, almost gristly muscle.

"You have enough curves." His eyes took in my body in a smooth, yet quick glance.

I think he could tell I was getting uncomfortable, because he shifted his eyes away from me and picked his shovel back up.

"Well, let's get this finished, shall we?" he asked.

Once again we shoveled in near silence, the clanging of our tools against hidden rocks and soft fall of the dirt our only soundtrack. It was getting too dark to see, and I heard a very soft roar of thunder a few miles away.

"Damn," I said. "We need to hurry, it'll be storming here soon. I'll run to the shed and grab my lights so we can see what we're doing."

Raphael's eyes widened. "Do you want me to come with you?"

"No, I'm fine, just keep digging." It was deep enough now that I had to pull myself out of the hole.

It only occurred to me after I walked away that Raphael might not have been comfortable being left by himself in a grave after dark. The thought made a cruel smile cross my lips, but at the same time I felt a bit guilty.

I brought back one of the big battery-operated lights; the light itself wasn't as good as electric, but with the storm coming I didn't want to waste time running cords. It would be enough to get finished.

Raphael looked relieved when I switched on the light.

"I'm sorry," I said to him.

"For what?" he asked.

"For leaving you in a grave in the dark. I forget that

would make most people uncomfortable." I jumped back in and started digging.

"You do this every day; I figured I would survive," he said.

The light helped, and I realized we were closer to being done than I had thought. It thundered again—this time, closer.

"Hurry," I said. "We need to be out of here before it rains too much, otherwise it's damn hard to get out of this hole."

He nodded and kept shoveling.

The rain started, just a drizzle at first. It was enough to cool us off and turn the dirt on our skin and clothes to mud.

I saw the first flash of lightning.

"OK, time to go," I said.

Moving to pull myself out of the grave, my hand slipped. I fell backwards, scraping my head on the edge of a rock I didn't see. My hand immediately went to my new wound as I sat there, stunned.

"Are you all right?" Raphael was leaning over me, offering a hand to help me up.

I nodded. "I think so." I took his hand.

He started to toss his shovel up on the side of the grave.

"Just leave it. We'll cover the shovels and the lamp with the tarps down here—that way we aren't carrying a bunch of metal back through the storm."

"That's smart," he said. "Here, let me give you a boost."

"I'm OK," I said reluctantly.

"Come on, there's no sense in not taking my help while I'm here."

I was being stubborn, but relented. I started to pull myself up, and he helped push my legs on up and out of the grave. He was out just a moment after me.

We stood there looking at each other a moment, only seeing shadows through the rain.

"Are you leaving?" I asked.

"Do you want me to?" he asked.

I knew the answer to that, but I wasn't sure I was supposed to say it.

"You can come back to the cabin for a shower, and wait until the storm passes," I offered, and felt my stomach flutter.

"That would be great," he said, and followed me.

We took off our boots on the porch and went inside.

"This is really nice," he said, looking around.

"It's small, but it's everything I need," I said.

"No, it's really cozy," he said as I turned on the fire.

"Do you want to shower first?" I offered. "There's a black robe hanging in the bathroom you can wear after, and I'll wash your clothes."

"That would be amazing," he smiled.

His face (and the rest of him) was covered with mud; somehow it only made his eyes seem even bluer.

I turned on the bathroom light, and he took the side of my face in his hand—I froze. *Is he going to kiss me?*

He turned my head toward the light, and I let him.

"You're bleeding," he said.

I touched the side of my neck, and came away with blood, streaked with dirt. "It's from that fall. It doesn't hurt too much."

He took a washcloth from the shelf and wet it with cold water. He gently wiped away the blood, and parted my hair so he could see the injury.

"You don't need stitches," he said as he kept the rag pressed to the side of my head and neck.

I was getting lightheaded, standing so long in one spot in the harsh light, so close to him. I put my hand over the rag and stepped back. I looked up at him and realized for the first time just how tall he really was.

I cleared my throat and forced myself to speak. "Thank you." I smiled. "Shower is all yours. Just toss out your dirty clothes."

He smiled back at me and gave a slight nod. There was a look in his eyes, though. It made me shiver.

He closed the door, and I walked into the kitchen to make a pot of tea for the two of us. I thought about the way his face looked with his hair pulled back. I wanted to trace his jawline with my fingertips. He was striking to look at. I bit my lip at the realization that I truly was attracted to him. It had only happened a few times before in real life; it was usually only characters in movies or the books I had read.

I put the tea leaves into the pot and filled it with hot water. While the tea steeped, I pulled two mugs from the shelf and set them down. Suddenly, I was aware of someone behind me.

I turned around to see Raphael there, his long black hair clung to his shoulders, wet from the shower. He was naked except for the white towel around his waist—his blue eyes like striking pieces of lapis.

I stared at him. My brain wasn't even attempting to think of words to say; my eyes were just taking in his beauty.

After several seconds of silence he smiled. "Where is your washing machine? I'll put these in."

My brain finally clicked back on, and I realized he

was holding his muddy wet clothes. "Oh, it's in the hall behind the closet doors."

"Thanks," he smiled. "Sorry, I didn't see the robe in the bathroom."

I remembered I had hung it in the back of the closet. It had been Ray's, and I'd had no use for it. I retrieved it and laid it on the back of the couch.

"Theres tea in the pot on the counter, if you'd like a cup. I'm going to get in the shower," I called as I walked into the bathroom.

I went to the trouble to brush my teeth and hair after my shower, realizing for a change that I cared at least a little about my appearance.

I put on the clean clothes I had brought into the bathroom with me, and walked out. Raphael had put on the robe and was sitting the chair nearest the fire drinking a cup of tea.

He looked over at me. "Feeling better?"

"Feeling cleaner," I said. "Aren't you burning up being near the fire? I only turned it on until we dried off a little."

"I can take the heat." He winked at me.

I smiled and poured myself a cup of tea. I sat down on the couch, a little farther from the flames.

He got out of his chair, walked over and sat down next to me.

"Tell me about yourself," he said.

"You already know more about me than I know about you," I said.

He nodded and sipped his tea. "What would you like to know?"

"Where are you from? How old are you? What do you do for a living?" I asked. "Those seem like good places to start."

"Kansas, twenty-five, and I get by with photography," he answered.

"What brought you to Virginia?"

"Just traveling, taking pictures… Trying to figure where I'm supposed to be," he said.

"And you've been on your own this whole time?"

"Well, I didn't start on my own." He shifted a little in his seat.

Something in his demeanor changed when he said that. A girlfriend, perhaps? My heart sank; of course a beautiful guy like this had a girlfriend.

"Who are—or were—you traveling with?" I hesitated on asking, but I was too curious.

"A couple of friends from college, and my girlfriend. We all made it as far as Indiana together. She decided she liked one of my friends better than me, and I continued exploring on my own." He shrugged, but I could see the memory was still a little tender.

Without thinking, I placed my hand on his leg. "I'm sorry."

He smiled and placed his hand over mine; it was warm and strong. "It is what it is. If bad stuff didn't happen, it couldn't lead us to good stuff."

I thought about that. I'd had plenty of death in my life, but I was almost numb to it at this point. Besides that, I just had the day to day: nothing great, nothing awful. It didn't seem like anything led me anywhere.

"So, Hel, what do you do around here when you aren't working?" he asked.

He moved his hand to sip his tea, so I moved mine; I was disappointed. "I read mostly, or listen to music. Sometimes I watch movies."

"What do you like to read?" he asked.

I pointed to a wall of books. "Well, I started with Ray's collection; that has everything from medical textbooks to horror novels to religious works. So I pretty much read everything. Ray insisted I be well read, and well rounded."

Raphael nodded, seeming quite impressed. "Music?"

"I guess what you would consider oldies. I grew up listening to the music Ray grew up on. I listen to newer music, too, but those are my favorites." I pointed to an old record player and stacks of vinyl.

His eyes lit up. "May I?"

I smiled. "You may."

He seemed quite focused going through the stacks of records, then pulled one out of the sleeve and put it on to play. I knew the song immediately: Sam Cooke's *Bring it On Home to Me.*

Raphael walked over to me and offered me his hand. I took it.

I had only ever danced with another guy like this, at my junior prom, and I hadn't liked him enough to give it much thought. But this, this guy, I was liking a lot. We danced around the cabin smiling at each other.

"You're a good dancer," he said.

"Ray taught me," I said. "I know I talk about him a lot, but he was the only person in my life for a long time. I mean, I've had boyfriends; I'm not a hermit. But he was the only consistent thing."

"Talk about him all you want." He spun me around and caught me off guard.

"And how did you learn to dance so well?" I asked. "I don't know of many guys that can do this."

"My parents wanted me to be well rounded too," he said.

I grinned and laid my head on his shoulder just as the song ended. I sighed and lifted my head. "That was nice."

"Another?" he asked as a new song played.

I glanced at the clock. It was after midnight. "I'd really love to, but it's getting late. I have to work tomorrow."

"Of course," he hesitated. "My clothes are finished washing, but still need to dry."

I laughed at my forgetfulness as he went to put them in the dryer.

"If you need to go to bed, I can wear the robe home and bring it back or something," he offered.

That was thoughtful.

"I'll be OK tomorrow," I said. "That's what coffee is for. Would you like to watch a movie while we wait?"

"Yes, that would be nice," he said.

I had lots of music, and lots of books, thanks to Ray; but I didn't have a big movie collection. It was a pretty fast decision for us to settle on The Lost Boys. I turned off the fire so the only light was a dim one coming from the bathroom.

We sat close to one another on the couch, and I was very aware of his body near mine. For a change, I was having trouble watching the movie. I just wanted to watch this person next to me, study his face and the curve of his shoulders. I tried not to stare too much. I didn't know what this was, or what to do next. It had been the only time in my adult life that I felt I needed a girlfriend to talk to.

About halfway into the movie, Raphael leaned

down to me and brushed my hair back behind my ear so he could ask, "Is it all right if I put my arm around you?"

My lungs refused to take in enough air to answer, so I simply nodded. He put his arm around me, and I sighed as I relaxed into his body. The softness of the robe brushed against my skin, and I could feel the firmness of his muscle underneath. The smell of soap and shampoo lingered on his skin and hair, but the products smelled different on him than they did me.

"You smell good," I whispered against him.

"So do you," he said against the top of my head.

This is what heaven feels like, I thought to myself as I drifted to sleep in his arms.

A loud sound in the movie caused me to startle awake. I focused my eyes to see a vampire screaming and dissolving in a bathtub of garlic water.

I was happily still nestled in close against Raphael. My neck had been leaning this way for too long and was starting to protest, but I desperately didn't want to move. I sat up against him and tried to stretch my head the other way. Without saying anything, he moved his arm and started massaging my neck. I let out a sound of pure enjoyment, and saw him smile.

After a few minutes I settled back against him. The movie was almost over, and I was already dreading watching him leave. I had already heard the dryer stop, so I knew his clothes were dry. I just really didn't want him to go.

"You can stay tonight if you want. I mean, it's already so late," I said, not believing what I was offering to this man I'd just met.

He was quiet; it made me nervous.

"I mean, you don't have to of course, but you're welcome to. Where are you staying in town, anyway?" I asked.

"I'm renting a little place in the valley," he replied. He still appeared to be thinking pretty hard.

I nodded.

"If I did stay, where would you want me to sleep?" he asked.

I swallowed past the tightness in my chest. "The couch is pretty comfortable, and then there is my bedroom. I, uh, can take the couch, or…" I hesitated, not knowing how to finish the sentence.

"Can I just be blunt with you for a minute?" he asked.

"Of course." My stomach was twisting inside of me.

"Before I left tonight, I was going to ask to kiss you." I smiled.

"But," he continued, "if I stay, I'm not going to."

I gave him the puzzled look I was feeling. "Why not?" My voice gave away more disappointment than I wanted it to.

He smiled. "Too much too soon. If I stay, I'll sleep on the couch; or if you want to cuddle, I'm good with that, but nothing more. So, you decide if I'm staying or not."

Well this was frustrating; not that I planned on having my way with him, or anything. But now that I knew he had wanted to kiss me—it changed things.

It was late, I had a cemetery to mow, and probably more graves to dig tomorrow. But I was already feeling wide awake after my little nap. I felt pretty certain that if he went home, and especially if he kissed me, I would be awake all night, anyway. Maybe if he stayed

I could let myself fall asleep. Yes, I was reaching, but it made me feel better.

He sat quietly with a serious look on his face, waiting for me to decide what I wanted tonight.

I looked at him and sighed. "Since you were blunt, I guess I can be too. I think it would be easier if you just stay tonight. That way you aren't having to walk back through the cemetery to your car, and getting to your place so late. But, I'll only let you stay on one condition." I stopped.

"What's that?" he questioned.

"If you aren't going to kiss me tonight, you have to come back and kiss me another time." I didn't look at him when I said it.

He laughed, and it was a warm sound that seemed to fill me up. "That, I can promise."

I stood up from the couch and stretched. "Come on, then. Let's get some sleep."

"Following you," he replied.

I turned off the TV that was still silently glowing blue after the movie had ended. Raphael followed me into my bedroom, and though I had never had a man in my room like this before, I was surprisingly comfortable with it. With my couple of ex-boyfriends, I always stayed with them, to spare Ray the discomfort. Even that hadn't felt as good as this.

Raphael, on the other hand, looked a little out of his element. I watched him look around my room, and he hesitated to move or touch anything without invitation.

"Which side of the bed do you want?" I asked.

"Which side do you normally sleep on?" he replied.

"All of it," I laughed. "Will you be comfortable

sleeping in the robe, or should I find you something?"

He ran his hands down the front of the robe. "This is fine."

I nodded and walked over to turn down the bed. The quilt was one of those generic cabin themes of plaid with little bears and trees thrown in. This had been Ray's bedroom, and I had had a twin, set up in the loft. When he died, I got rid of the twin and took the larger room. It seemed like the only reasonable thing to do.

A small part of me wondered how Ray would feel about me having a man over here, staying the night in his old bed. I could imagine him shaking his head and smiling at me for finally doing something a little out of routine. He'd always had good things to say about love, in spite of his failed marriage... not that this was love. But I hoped it was something.

Once again, I had let my thoughts carry me a bit too far away. I heard Raphael clear his throat, and snapped out of my head long enough to see him waiting for me in bed. My heart sped up enough to make me nervous that he would be able to feel it, and that only made it beat harder. I smiled at him and turned off the lights. I walked over and crawled into bed with him. My bed was already so much warmer than when it was only me getting in for the night.

He was on one side, and I was on the other; the space between our bodies seemed like miles. I couldn't sleep like this; I wanted him close. I slowly inched my way towards him until I could feel the edge of his body against mine.

"Comfy?" I asked.

"Oh yeah, this is great," he said, and I heard him

yawn.

"Good," I replied, still frustrated. I didn't know whether I should stay facing him, or turn my back towards him so he could wrap his arms around me, if he ever would.

I kept moving and shifting in the bed, trying to get closer or get comfortable. I thought I was being subtle, but after a few minutes Raphael spoke up.

"You're not used to sharing your bed, are you?" he laughed.

"Sorry," I said.

"It's fine; you need sleep though. I'll take the couch." He started to get up, and I grabbed his hand.

"Please stay in here. I just want to be closer to you," I quickly blurted out before he could leave.

My heart must have decided my brain was no longer allowed to think through what I was going to say, and somehow short circuited it. I was quite surprised at myself once the words were out. He squeezed my hand and got back in bed, pulling me close against him so that my head was on his chest and my fingers were in his hair. We both sighed, and then, we slept.

CHAPTER THREE

When I woke up the next morning, he was still there—an oil spill of black hair across my light green sheets. I ran my fingers through it as I had done the night before.

The light through the window was just enough that I knew it was probably nearly 7:00AM. My bedside clock agreed with me. I needed to get up, make breakfast, and get busy before the day got too hot again. Thankfully, I hadn't gotten any calls yet for more graves. That thought reminded me that I needed to check the one we had worked on last night to make sure it was done.

I looked at Raphael again and my head felt light and giddy, but at the same time my chest felt heavy and sad at the thought of him leaving today.

I wondered if I should wake him up, or if I should get up and fix breakfast for the two of us. I hadn't cooked for anyone except Ray. He had thought my cooking was pretty good. I could make coffee, and pancakes, and bacon.

Once more I looked at the man in my bed; he was beautiful. Women probably begged him to come home with them most nights, and yet here he was, in my bed, after spending his evening helping me dig a grave.

Slowly, and carefully I rolled out of bed, and sighed with relief when I looked back to see him still asleep. I put my hair up and made my way to the kitchen.

I started the coffee first, so I could drink a cup while I cooked. I had never realized how much noise everything makes when you're trying to be quiet.

I hummed the song we had danced to the night before, and was smiling stupidly as I poured pancake batter into the hot skillet.

"Good morning."

I jumped and turned around to see Raphael standing at the counter. "You startled me."

"Sorry." He yawned and stretched. His eyes were still heavy with sleep.

I could tell he wasn't a morning person.

"Could I get my clothes?" he asked.

"Sure. They're still in the dryer," I said.

He shuffled off through the cabin to change, and came back a few minutes later in his torn jeans and black t-shirt. I already missed him in just the robe.

"Can you stay for breakfast? It's almost ready," I invited.

He was quiet for a minute. "Uh, sure, I can do that. I just don't want to keep you if you need to work."

"Well I have to eat, too," I smiled. I realized I was probably entirely too perky for him this early. I'd try to tone it down.

"Coffee?" I asked.

"Please."

"Cream and sugar?" I offered.

"Just black."

I poured and handed him a cup, then jumped back to the skillet to get the pancake out before it burned.

"Can I help?" he asked.

"I got it, thanks though," I said.

We ate breakfast, but didn't talk as much as I had hoped. It made me a little uncomfortable and afraid I had imagined all the chemistry between us the night before.

We finished eating, and he helped me clean up the dishes. Afterwards, he walked out onto the porch and put on his boots. I knew what was coming next, and I dreaded it.

"I guess I should be going," he said. "Thanks for letting me stay, and for washing my clothes, and making me breakfast," he laughed.

"Thanks for helping me work last night, and for staying with me. I haven't had company in a long time. It was nice." I stood in front of him on the porch, feeling a bit awkward. "Am I going to see you again?" I asked, continuing our bluntness from the night before.

"I owe you that kiss, right?" He gave a slight smile.

I felt the butterflies start in my stomach again. "I think that was the deal."

"Then yes, you will see me again." He smiled and gave a slight wave as he walked off towards the cemetery.

I watched him walk away and wished I had at least hugged him goodbye. I had spent the night in his arms, why was touching him suddenly awkward? I guess what happens in the dark feels different in the day.

He left, and I worked. I mowed and weeded and

removed old dead flower arrangements from the tombstones. I made sure last night's grave was ready for the woman's burial, and by the time I had finished all of my work, I could see the sun starting to sink behind the mountains.

I had ridden a roller-coaster of feelings all day. I tried to stay focused and not think about Raphael and all the possibilities with him. And then, I'd switch and remember as many details as I could from the night before, trying to feel all the tingles and butterflies of being close to him.

I went through my evening routine hoping to hear a knock at the door, and at some point, I surrendered to sleep.

It was three days before I saw him again.

I was trimming some shrubs out by the gate when I saw his Jeep parked at the far end of the lot. I looked around but didn't see him. It felt odd: if he didn't want to see me, why was he back again; and if he did, why wasn't he here?

I finished cutting branches and cleaned up the mess. As I walked back toward the shed, I saw Raphael: he was standing over a grave. His shoulders were shaking gently, and he dropped his head as he placed his hand on the gravestone.

It was pretty clear he had had another reason for visiting my cemetery. My heart immediately broke for him. I mapped out the cemetery in my mind, trying to place whose stone that was. It had been somewhere around a year since Ray and I had dug that grave. 'Stephanie?' Was that the name? I tried to picture the gravestone in my mind. I always felt a little bad when I couldn't remember a name or cause of death, even though that wasn't really part of my job. I felt like I should know the people in my cemetery.

Raphael looked up and saw me, his face wet with silent tears. I just stood there, not sure if he wanted me to come closer, or let him mourn in peace.

He forced a smile and waved. I walked over.

He didn't say anything when I stood beside him. We both looked down, contemplating the plot in front of us. After a moment he broke the silence.

"Did you dig her grave?" he asked.

"Ray and I did, together," I said softly.

I noticed the dates on the stone and immediately remembered the funeral. Ray and I weren't always around during the graveside services unless we were tending something nearby. We had been that day, planting flowers I believe. It stood out because of how loud the crying was; it had been a suicide. Those funerals always stuck with you.

"How did you know her?" I asked, and put my hand on his shoulder.

"She went to college with me, she was one of my best friends." He touched the stone again.

"Did you date?"

"We hooked up a few times, but she never wanted anything too serious." There was so much sadness in his eyes.

I was trying to piece together the things I knew about him, and how this fit in. "The road trip you were on with friends, were you all coming here to see her?"

He nodded. "We had all been good friends. Stephanie had always tried to tell me Anna had a crush on me. I got together with her after Steph died; we wanted to come say goodbye." He put his hand over my hand on his shoulder. "Do you know what happened?" he asked, and I could hear the tightness in his voice, forcing the words out.

"I don't know the circumstances, but I know how she died," I said.

His shoulders stiffened and his voice lost some emotion it had held. "No one really knows the circumstances. She didn't talk to anyone."

Anger… So much hurt and anger for being left behind without a goodbye.

I took his hand in mine and squeezed it gently.

"Do you want a beer?" I offered.

He smiled at me. "Yeah," he sighed, and turned away from her grave.

We sat on my porch, each sipping a Sam Adams and looking over the quiet rolling green hills dotted with gray headstones. The mountains in the distance were tall and green.

"Why didn't you tell me the other night?" I asked.

"I don't know," he shrugged. "It just never seemed like the right time."

"Loss is hard; it doesn't have to make sense. Has coming back given you any sort of closure?" I asked.

"I think only an explanation could do that." He took a swig of his beer and brushed back a few strands of hair that had escaped his ponytail.

I didn't know what to say to that, so I sipped my beer and said nothing.

"I'm sorry," he said.

"For what?" I asked.

"For not telling you everything the other day, and for being a downer today."

I laughed. "It's not an easy thing to talk about,

especially just meeting someone. And you know I live in a cemetery and dig graves for a living. It's hard to bring me down. I just want you to be OK."

He took my hand in his and looked at me. "Meeting you has been the only part of my trip that's made this OK."

Those damn butterflies again.

We chatted more about my job and how I had gotten to be where I was. I told him about the trips Ray and I had taken around the U.S. Ray wanted me to know there was more to this world than our little corner, our little graveyard. I had been particularly taken with Colorado and Montana: I liked the open skies with mountains. He had insisted I go to college, even though I knew I wanted to take over for him. He wasn't thrilled when I went for a business degree; Ray believed skills were most important. Also, we knew several people in town working for minimum wage with business degrees. But I managed to convince him it wasn't totally worthless away from our small town.

I talked and talked to Raphael, telling him about my life; I couldn't recall anyone ever being that interested before.

"Have you had any serious boyfriends?" Raphael asked sometime during my rambling.

"Sure, I've had boyfriends in the past but none lasted long. Most men don't like a woman who does more physical labor than they do, and my job creeps them out. I had one semi-serious boyfriend in college a couple of years ago. He was studying mortuary science, so he wasn't bothered by the job," I said, remembering the guy's wide brown eyes and pasty skin.

"What happened?" he asked.

"He got weird, which, in our line of work, says something," I laughed. "He started picking up roadkill, and cutting himself for fun. He asked if he could cut me during sex one night, and then asked if we could have sex in an open grave. I guess I'm not that kinky."

Raphael made a face that clearly showed how warped that sounded. "Good call on letting that one go." He held up his beer in acknowledgment.

I laughed.

Raphael put his hand on my knee, and asked, "So, do you have a lot more work today?"

"I just need to water the flowers and give everything a walk through," I said.

"How about I help you do that, and then you let me take you out for dinner?" he asked.

I couldn't remember the last time I had been on a real date, or eaten inside a restaurant in town. It had been before Ray died.

"That sounds great." I smiled at him.

Raphael helped me finish up my chores, and sat on the couch while I got ready. I was as fast in the shower as I could be, still taking the time to shave my legs and everything else.

I put on more makeup than I usually wore (the usual amount being none), and blow dried my hair so that it was full and silky down my back.

I rummaged through my closet for the first time in ages, since I was used to grabbing the same work clothes from the floor or dryer every morning. I couldn't even remember what I might have that would be nice for dinner. Finally, I found a little black summer dress with spaghetti straps and a flowing skirt. It was a little on the short side but I would be careful to keep it pulled down. As it turned out, finding a dress was easier than finding shoes. Boots—so many boots— one pair of sneakers, an old pair of blue flip flops… *Dammit.* I was about to give up when I remembered I had a bag of clothes to get rid of, things I had worn at college that I didn't want anymore. I had meant to take the bag to our local women's shelter for ages, but now I was glad I hadn't. I dug around in the white trash bag until my fingers wrapped around a pair of black strappy sandals with silver clasps. *Thank God.*

I looked at myself in the mirror and hardly recognized myself. I definitely needed to clean up more often; it was nice feeling sexy and girly.

I walked out of the bedroom, suddenly self-conscious when his eyes fell on me.

"Sorry I took so long," I muttered. "I couldn't find any shoes."

His eyes were taking me in so slowly and completely I wanted to cover myself up.

"You look beautiful."

I smiled. "Thank you."

He walked over to me. "Ready?"

I nodded.

We walked outside, and he took my arm. "Where would you like to go?"

"We don't have too many options." I thought for a moment. "Do you have a preference?"

"Lets go to the restaurant in the hotel just outside of town. They have decent food and pretty good drinks, and they have a nice atmosphere."

"Sounds good," I agreed.

We drove a while listening to music; it was either a very new or obscure band, because I didn't recognize them at all. I was still immensely enjoying being with Raphael, but putting the label of date on this was making me a little less comfortable around him. I hadn't been on a date in so long—not since my last "odd" boyfriend.

Once we arrived at the restaurant, Raphael dashed around to help me out of the car and offer his arm once more. He knew how capable I was from day to day, so for him to offer his arm to me for any added comfort seemed exceptionally sweet.

The restaurant wasn't super fancy, by any means, but it was nice enough that I put my napkin on my lap and tried to keep my elbows off the table.

"Wine?" Raphael asked.

"Always," I agreed with enthusiasm.

We settled on a zinfandel called Seven Deadly Zins, and ordered steaks to go with it. While we were waiting on our food, we sipped our wine and I looked around the room. Raphael was right, this place did have a nice atmosphere. The walls were the color of rich dark honey, and the lighting accentuated it. A little vase of red flowers had been placed on every table, along with a small tea light candle. Classical violin music played overhead. It was all very mood setting.

Once my eyes finished wandering, they came back to Raphael—who was watching me so intensely I nearly jumped.

"What?" I asked.

"Nothing, I just think you're really beautiful," he said.

I felt my face heat up, no doubt accentuated by the wine. I took another sip. "Thanks," I said, looking away from him.

"Why does me calling you beautiful make you uncomfortable?" He raised an eyebrow and looked genuinely concerned.

I had to stop and ask myself, 'Why did it make me uncomfortable?'

In my silence he asked, "Has no one ever told you that before?"

I nodded. "Ray, told me all the time, and I've heard it from others. Girls always think I'm too muscular," I said again. I blushed once more when I realized what I thought to be the reason his words made me shaky. "I think the reason it makes me feel weird when you say it is because I've never been called beautiful by someone that I find so beautiful." Somehow, I managed get the words past the enormous lump in my throat.

His eyes absolutely danced with the compliment, and he smiled, showing his very white, pretty teeth. As soon as he was overtaken by the emotion, though, he regained his composure, going back to more of a 'hmm, that is very interesting' kind of look.

"Thank you," he said. "I don't think I've ever been called beautiful. Handsome, yes, charming, attractive, but not beautiful."

"Those fit you too, but I said beautiful because of the way your hair falls against your back and shoulders— the way your eyes are always the coldest deep blue, but still manage to be warm. And your face… you are undoubtedly masculine, but you are beautiful." As soon as I stopped talking, I glared at my wine glass thinking, *You made me do this.*

He took the hand that was resting on my glass, pulled it to his lips, and laid the gentlest of kisses on the back of it. It was light and delicate, with the feel of his warm breath on my skin. I closed my eyes as a chill ran through me. I really wanted him to kiss me tonight.

Our food came, and we talked about a little of everything as we ate and finished off the wine.

The waiter came back. "Dessert?"

Raphael ordered two pieces of chocolate cheesecake to go.

I looked at him, and he said, "To have with coffee back at your place."

I smiled and nodded.

There was more tension in the air as we drove back to my house. We had moved past the "interested friends" phase, and on to the "please let me get my hands on this person" phase. At least, that's what I was feeling.

Once in the house, Raphael set the cheesecake down on the counter, and I started putting on a pot of coffee. I felt him come up behind me and place his hands on the sides of my hips pulling them back against him. I sighed against him and started to turn around.

He leaned in and whispered against my ear, "Go ahead and finish what you're doing."

I put the filter in the basket and was trying to count out scoops of coffee, when he brushed my hair back and kissed my neck.

I started to turn to him once more, but his hand on my waist held firm. "Ugh." I hurriedly added the water. I turned to him, and this time he let me.

He took my face in his hands, and I looked into

those deep ocean eyes. He kissed me hard and fiercely, pressing me back into the counter. I opened my mouth to him and he took everything I gave him. He kissed me like he was starving. I tasted the red wine on his lips and I drank him down.

He pulled back, leaving me breathless. My fingers were still wrapped in his hair, and his were tangled in mine. He kissed me quickly and smiled. "Ready for dessert?"

I stared at him blankly for a minute, trying to determine if he was talking about sex. I must have looked confused.

"Do you want to grab plates or pour coffee?" he asked.

"I uhh, I'll grab plates. Not sure I should be handling hot liquids right now," I said, still a little shaky.

He grinned at me.

CHAPTER FOUR

We ate our cheesecake sitting on the living room floor, while Raphael played some of Ray's old records.

"Have you ever thought about leaving here and doing something else?" he asked.

I shrugged. "Ray always told me I could be anything I wanted, and I guess with my degree I could live anywhere. It's just, this is home, and I like digging graves and tending to the cemetery. I know I might not do it forever, but I can while I'm able."

Raphael nodded and took a bite of his cheesecake. I watched his tongue lick a missed bit off of his lips and wished he'd kiss me again.

"Why do you ask?" I said.

"Just curious. I thought you might like to take a break and travel with me for a while," Raphael said.

The statement caught me off guard. "Travel where?"

"Wherever we want." He winked a blue eye at me.

"For how long?" I asked.

"A weekend, a few weeks, a few months. As long as you want," he said.

"Are you planning to leave soon?" I stared at him,

now concerned.

"I don't know. I can't sit still long, but I like your company, so I might stay." Raphael's eyes locked with mine.

I didn't like him leaving, but I also didn't like the idea of giving up everything I had ever known to travel with someone I barely knew.

"A weekend?" I asked again.

"Sure, we can start there." His eyes were bright. "Where would you like to go?"

I thought about it. "I haven't seen the ocean since I was a little girl."

"When do you want to leave?" he asked.

"Next weekend," I suggested. That would give me time to arrange another caretaker while I was away. I hadn't asked for a vacation since before Ray died, so I didn't think anyone would be too upset.

"Perfect." Raphael smiled and leaned to kiss me again.

The little kiss led to more kisses, which led to him pulling me into his lap with my legs wrapped around his body.

"Can I stay again tonight?" he asked.

I knew this time there would be more than cuddling if he stayed. I was pretty sure I was good with that.

"Yes, I'd like that," I said. "I can't stay up too late, though. I have a lot to do this week if I'm going away with you."

"Could I help you? I'd be happy to pitch in this week, digging, mowing, whatever you need." He intertwined his fingers with mine and kissed them.

"I guess I could pay you as extra help," I mused.

"You don't have to pay me." He rolled his eyes.

I leaned in and kissed him. "Let's go to bed."

"Yes, I'd like that," he said.

I went into the bathroom to brush my teeth and hair before getting into bed with Raphael. My instincts were all over the place. I hadn't known him long and was already taking him to bed? Again? The mirror reflected a concerned 'oops' face, which made me giggle, and then roll my eyes and turn away from it.

True, I hadn't known Raphael long, but how well did we ever know anyone? I felt like I knew him better after two days spent together than months with other people. My last boyfriend (the weird one), I had known for several months before we dated, and longer before we slept together. He ended up being psycho, and stalked me for six months after everything ended. He seemed great at first, too. You never know crazy people are crazy if they didn't want you to know.

I thought about the next weekend: about lying on the beach with Raphael listening to the waves and seagulls, walking the boardwalk with him and eating funnel cake, staying buzzed on daiquiris and margaritas. It sounded perfect.

I emerged from the bathroom feeling a little nervous, and a lot excited, to get into bed with Raphael. He was on the same side of the bed as before, and had turned on the bedside lamp. He was propped up against the pillows wearing only his black boxer briefs. His skin was smooth and muscled, and his beautiful hair was down, spilling across his shoulders. Maybe I was imagining it, but I swear I could see the color of his eyes from across the room.

"I was planning to sleep in my underwear. Hope you don't mind," he said

I stood in the doorway, still taking it all in. "I don't mind a bit."

Raphael patted the bed beside him. "Are you joining me?"

I smiled, walked over to the bed, and got beneath the covers beside him. I had traded my clothes and underwear for a short silky pajama outfit.

My legs were barely in the bed before Raphael was leaning over me. He was staring at me intently once more. "Beautiful," he said.

The warmth from his body was already making me want to move in closer to him. I put my hand on the back of his neck and pulled him down towards me while I raised up to meet his kiss. He kissed me deeply, and my body moved beneath the covers to find the rest of his. I needed to feel his whole body pressed against mine. He obliged, and moved so that he was directly on top of me, his mouth still locked to mine. The weight of him pressing on me was heavier than I expected, and I could feel the extra effort in my lungs to take a deep breath, but it was good. It was so good. He pulled away from the kiss and I stared into his eyes, this time feeling more bold than I had. He smiled at me, a look of pure contentment meeting my gaze of desire.

"This is getting intense," he said.

"Mhm." I could feel my breath shallow and fast against his chest.

"I just want to be clear. Do you want to have sex tonight?" He smoothed my hair back behind my ear, and his fingers brushed the side of my face.

I didn't think I had ever had anyone ask me so bluntly: in the past with my two exes it had just kind of happened, even with the first one. It was kind of nice to be asked how far I wanted things to go, and not just assumed because we were sharing a bed.

"This isn't a one-night thing is it?" I asked. I hadn't even realized that was a concern until I asked the question.

He smiled down at me and kissed me. "No. I mean I don't know where this is going in the future, but I don't want it to be a one-night thing."

"Then yes, I do want to have sex with you tonight," I said.

Soon we were both naked, and he smiled and leaned back down to kiss me. He kissed me lightly at first, and then slowly went deeper to explore my mouth with his tongue as his fingers explored my body. He kissed my neck and made little nips along my skin with his teeth. He traced every line of my body with his tongue and kisses, until my skin was so sensitive even the lightest touch from him made me sigh and shiver.

"Please, enough," I gasped, and jumped as he grazed his teeth along the edge of my hip. He looked up at me and grinned.

"Enough? You're finished? Ok." He rolled off of me. "Goodnight then."

"Ah," I groaned. "Get back over here." I reached over and ran my fingers down his chest and stomach, to things lower.

This time Raphael moaned. That was all the motivation I needed. I took my turn of showering his body in kisses and nibbles and soft touches. I only made it to his stomach before he grabbed me and flipped me on my back. The table lamp was still on and we could see each other well. He was on his knees between my legs looking down at me.

Seeing him look down at me with so much need in his eyes almost scared me, but I wanted him more than I had ever wanted anyone.

"This is my favorite part," he said.

I watched him slide on the condom he had laid on the table. I looked at him, waiting for more.

"The moment you know it's getting ready to happen: the anticipation of how good you will feel to me, and how good I will feel to you, and being as close as we can be." He slowly pushed into me and I closed my eyes.

"No." He stopped. "Look at me." His fingers brushed my face.

I opened my eyes and gripped his arms as he moved again. He was bigger than the other two men I had been with, and if he hadn't warmed me up so well, it would have hurt. It didn't hurt though; he filled me completely, and I loved it.

"Are you ok?" he asked.

"You feel amazing," I said.

He kissed me and found his rhythm. He moved me from position to position effortlessly, letting my body take him in at all angles. Some didn't work yet because of his size, but once I was used to being with him, we could try again.

"You haven't come yet," he said, nuzzling my neck.

"I usually don't during sex. It's ok, you still feel amazing," I said.

He shook his head and made a grumpy face. "No, it's not. What do you want me to do?"

I shrugged. "I don't know what it would take."

He looked thoughtful for a moment, then grabbed the pillow from the other side of the bed. "Lift your hips," he said.

I did, and he placed the pillow underneath me. He slid back inside me, and I made a little sound again. His body moved, and I could tell this felt very different. He kept his rhythm steady, and I felt the pressure building.

I let out a cry against his chest as I came. He kissed me and continued to move, building to his own release. It was too much to feel him still hitting that tender spot while I was still shaking inside.

I bit my lip, and tried to say, "Raphael," to stop him just so I could move the pillow, but he went harder and faster so that all that came out of my mouth was a scream. I wrapped my legs around him as I came again, this time with him.

We both laid there, sweaty and satisfied, next to each other. Raphael's hand found mine and squeezed it. "You *can* orgasm during sex."

"Huh. I guess I can," I laughed.

Raphael joined me in the shower the next morning, and though it was tempting to have him again, we refrained so I could get to work.

"I'll run out and get us some breakfast, and then I can help you when I get back." He kissed me as he got ready to go out the door.

"Ok, that sounds great." I was relieved. When we had gotten up that morning, I had two messages for side-by-side plots that needed to be dug: car accident.

While Raphael went to get us some food, I got the tools out of the shed and marked off the grave-sites. It would be so nice to have help. I could dig two in three days' time, but it really was too much for one person.

I didn't want to start digging and getting sweaty until I had something to eat. If I got weak and shaky from low blood sugar (more possible after last night's activities), it would take me hours to recover. I didn't have time for that.

So, I walked the cemetery. I checked the front gate, made sure the flowers on the headstones weren't wilted or turned over, pulled a few weeds, and noted which statues needed to be cleaned of bird poop.

I walked by the newest grave in the cemetery: it was the grave Raphael had first helped me with. Her funeral had gone pretty smoothly, but there weren't as many people as one would expect for a young woman's funeral. I shrugged, thinking about how few people would be at mine if I died. Maybe the woman had just been an introvert.

Something odd in the dirt caught my attention. I had packed down and smoothed the dirt once the coffin had been lowered into the grave. Now, looking down at it, it looked as though it hadn't been touched, but something shiny was peeking out. I leaned over and pulled it out: it was a sterling silver bracelet.

I knew there was no way I could have missed something that shiny hiding in the dirt while I was shoveling it into the grave. It was unlikely that someone, say a friend or family member, had brought it after the funeral. Why would they only bury a part of it, and then smooth the surrounding ground?

Ray always said if anything, no matter how small,

seemed unusual or strange about a grave, to always take precautions. So, even though I still didn't understand his superstitions, I did what I knew he would have wanted.

I went to the cabin and got a big can of salt, a small bottle of olive oil, a bottle of some Florida water given to us by a hoodoo man, and three iron nails. He kept these things together in a special box in the closet. Only three times, that I could recall, had he ever used them, and I had only done it once before now. I was a little embarrassed the first time I did it alone. The blood I thought I had seen on a headstone had turned out to be poop from a bird that had eaten berries.

I still felt silly, but I made my way back through the cemetery and looked at the grave. I had laid the bracelet on top of the headstone before walking to the house, I was positive. It was gone now. I looked all around the headstone in the grass, and glanced all around the cemetery for someone who might have taken it. No one was there, and there were no cars in the parking lot.

Raphael pulled in while I was still trying to figure out what the hell was going on. He saw me, and came walking up carrying two Burger King bags.

"What's wrong?" he asked.

I had my finger to my lips, looking at the grave and then looking around again.

"Remember the first day you asked me if I had ever seen anything weird or unexplainable, and I didn't really answer you?" I asked.

He nodded.

"Well it's very rare—extremely rare—but sometimes odd things happen with graves. Ray claimed to have seen ghosts or spirits at night once or twice, or grass wouldn't grow over a new grave because the ground kept getting disturbed; and once, dead animals kept showing up on the grave, like an offering. With the last one, we thought maybe it was someone practicing black magic, or a crazy person. But we set up a camera, and it was animals bringing their prey and leaving it on the grave. We don't know what any of it means, except we can only assume that somehow the person's spirit isn't at rest," I said.

"That's really bizarre," he said staring down at the grave. "So what's wrong with this one, and what do you do?"

I told him what I had found, and how the bracelet had disappeared. Then I took the three iron nails and pushed them as deeply as I could down into the earth, over what would be just above the head, stomach, and feet. "This ties the spirit to the grave so it can't wander."

Then I poured a dash of Florida water on a rag and wiped the headstone down, followed by making a cross on the top of the stone with the olive oil while I said Psalm 23.

"This cleanses and blesses the grave," I told him.

Lastly, I took the salt and made a circle around the grave. "This protects the grave and spirit from any evil."

"Do you believe this works?" Raphael asked once I was done.

"Nothing else strange usually happens once it's done. Ray was a pretty logical man: he liked to know how things worked, but he also said, 'Just because you don't understand something doesn't make it wrong.'

So I do it."

"He sounded pretty smart," Raphael smiled.

I nodded. I missed him.

"Food?" Raphael asked.

"Yes, please," I said, and walked back to the cabin.

I put away the special supplies, and poured cups of coffee and orange juice for us to drink while we ate breakfast on the porch.

We ate quickly and almost silently. My mind was stuck on the disturbed grave. Could people reach out from the dead?

Ray had taught me about religions growing up, and he'd taught me about evolution. He followed no particular religion, but he talked to me about God and Jesus and Buddha and all the others. He encouraged me to study everything and follow what made sense.

I thought I believed in some kind of higher power, but life after death was a tough one for me to buy. I wanted to believe Ray was somewhere wonderful— "Heaven," if you will… But did I really believe it? I wasn't sure.

"Sure you're OK?" Raphael eyed me while I ate my biscuits and sausage gravy.

"Sorry, I'm fine." I took another bite and a sip of coffee.

The sky was blue tinged with gray, but it was cloudless and the sun wasn't trying very hard to scorch us yet. I felt just a sliver of autumn in the air. Not true fall that shows in the blueness of the sky, this was just a whisper of her in the breeze.

"Do you still want to go to the beach next weekend?" Raphael asked.

That broke me out of my trance. "Yes!" I leaned over

and kissed him. "I can't wait."

He smiled at me, and I thought about how I would never tire of looking into his eyes. I leaned in and he kissed me again—this time, more than a peck on the lips.

I pulled away, this time leaving him breathless.

"So, we need to go inside for a little while before we work..." There was a mischievous grin on his face.

I played innocent. "Why would that be?"

"I, uh, need to show you something in the bedroom," he said tugging on my hand.

I shook my head. "Sorry, it will have to wait until tonight. There is work to be done."

He made a pouty face at me. "Fine, let's get to it. Chop-chop, and all that."

I laughed, and we got busy.

We dug for four hours before we stopped for a break. I had more done than Raphael, but he did well at trying to keep pace. We covered each grave with a tarp and went back to the cabin.

I got two glasses down from the shelf and mixed up water with an electrolyte supplement. I handed Raphael a glass and drank my own. He drank it, but made an unhappy face.

"It really helps," I reassured him.

"We're only halfway finished and my whole body hurts," he said, stretching his arms back behind him, and then rubbing his shoulders. "No wonder you're in such good shape."

I smiled. "Digging is a good workout, but it's repetitive, so you have to move your body in an opposite way to balance it out. I have certain stretches I do every day."

"Show me," he said rubbing at his back.

"I can't in work clothes," I said, but I took an ice pack out of the freezer and tossed it to him. "This should help for now."

He sighed in relief as he placed the ice pack against his back.

I was fumbling around the kitchen, throwing things away and picking up here or there. I still wasn't sure what I was supposed to be doing while he was around. I was so used to it just being me.

"Do I make you nervous?" he questioned, and raised an eyebrow again as he watched me zipping around.

"No, not nervous. I just don't know what to do with myself while you're here." I quickly followed that with, "But I love having you here."

"As long as you want me here. Promise you'll tell me if you need a break from me. I don't want to overstay my welcome." He walked towards me.

"I promise," I said when his face was only inches from mine. How did this gorgeous man want to be with *me*?

"Good," he said, closing the distance from his lips to mine. He kissed me, and I leaned in against him with my fingers playing in his hair. Suddenly something freezing was pressed against the skin on my back: the ice pack. I half gasped, half screamed against his mouth and tried to push him away.

"Shh," Raphael said as he nipped at my neck and ear.

I sank against him and found his lips once more. He dropped the ice pack and I felt his fingers working at the buttons of my jeans.

"Raphael, I'm so sweaty and gross." I put my hand

over his and shook my head at him.

"So am I," he leaned in and whispered, "but do you really want to stop me?"

I bit my lip, "No, not really. But we need to work," I argued again.

"I bet we can be fast," he said, and moved my hand out of the way to finish taking off my jeans.

I was suddenly half naked in the kitchen. I stepped out of the jeans and looked at him. It was always unnerving to be the only one in the room missing clothes.

His fingers traced along the outline of my panties, and the feeling made my legs begin to shake. It felt too good. I closed my eyes and let my head fall against his chest. He kept touching me until my legs were shaking harder and my breathing was coming heavy. He stopped, and I whined against him.

"Nope, gotta get back to work," he said.

"Ugh, you enormous tease!" I relented, shoving against his chest in frustration, and snapping up my jeans from the floor.

We finished the graves before dark, and I walked by the odd grave I'd done the ritual on earlier. All appeared well.

Raphael held my hand as I did my evening walk-through around the cemetery. I made a mental note that a few shrubs needed to be trimmed the next day, and some dead flowers taken away. Tomorrow would be an easy work day.

I walked by Ray's grave and told him goodnight,

and gave a passing wave to my parents. Raphael paused near the grave of his friend.

"Do you need a minute?" I squeezed his hand.

He was stiff and his expression was blank. "I just can't believe she left us like that."

"It's ok to be angry with her. Some days I'm still angry with my dad, even though I loved Ray more than I can say. But don't hold onto it. Be angry, then let it go, even if it comes back." I wrapped my arm around his waist and hugged him.

He nodded, still looking at the grave. "Not today."

The rolling green hills of the cemetery were fading as the dark was drawing in.

"Are you staying with me again tonight," I queried, "or are you tiring of me?"

"Definitely not," he said.

"You're definitely not staying with me?" I was a little disappointed.

"No! Damn, I mean I'm definitely not tired of you. I want to stay. I have more clothes in my car," he laughed.

"You were prepared!" I laughed.

"Some days I just drive and end up far away. I've learned to be prepared," he said.

We walked into the house and I turned on the lights. I really needed to clean, Raphael was a distraction, or I was a little obsessive in my housekeeping—not sure of which.

Raphael sat on a stool at the bar in the kitchen. "Can I have another ice pack?"

"This time a hot shower would be better," I said.

"I'm too tired for a shower. Will you take one with me?" He tried to look pitiful.

"I will, but I'm too tired for any extra shower activities," I smiled.

He actually stuck out his lip in a pout. I walked over and kissed him.

"Maybe fun shower activities tomorrow?" I asked.

He pressed his lips to mine in a hard-but-silly movement. "Yes."

We did shower together. I washed his hair and body and he washed mine. We were tender and gentle with one another, laughing a few times when I nearly slipped out of the tub.

I appreciated the beauty of his body all slick and soapy, but my body ached, and I knew if we had any more fun, I'd be too exhausted to function tomorrow.

We dried off, put on robes, and made sandwiches in the kitchen. We watched a movie on the couch while we ate our sandwiches and drank a beer. Then we crawled in bed together, and he held me while I slept. Him, this… it was everything.

CHAPTER FIVE

THE NEXT MORNING, I GOT UP BEFORE RAPHAEL and made coffee. I called into town to let them know I'd be gone the following weekend. No one seemed to mind; they said they'd have someone come by and check in on everything while I was gone, and they knew who to call if a grave had to be dug while I was away.

I cringed a little, knowing that meant they'd call the guy with the heavy machinery, but dammit, I couldn't do everything.

Raphael got up shortly after I made my phone calls, and we mixed up a batch of blueberry muffins to go in the oven while we talked about our beach trip. He pulled up pictures of the hotels on his phone, and we found a reasonable one right on the beach.

"I can take you dancing at night, and we can be beach bums during the day." He kissed my cheek and placed a muffin on my plate.

I smiled: it sounded perfect.

"I think I'm going to go back to my place today," Raphael mused and sipped his coffee.

Not wanting to sound needy, I said, "Ok, if you have

to."

He touched my hand, "I just need to get my laptop and camera, and more clean clothes."

To be honest, I needed to do laundry myself, and clean my house. "You'll come back tonight?"

"Mhm," he nodded. "You don't have to dig today, do you?"

"Nope, everything in the cemetery is good today besides just a walk through. I think I'll clean the house while you're gone."

He walked into the bedroom and put his things in his bag. He kissed me before he left, and I missed his presence the minute he walked out the door. The L-word crossed my mind, but I quickly hushed it. This was much too soon... right?

I cleaned the house in record time trying to keep myself busy. Then, I showered and painted my toenails. I was surprised I could even find a bottle of nail polish, it had been so long since I had used any.

The house was clean, I was clean, and it was still hours before Raphael would be back. I started thinking about what I would pack for the beach. A look through my closet quickly showed me shopping was in order.

I heard a knock at my door and went to open it, expecting to greet Raphael with a kiss. It wasn't Raphael standing there, though: it was a delivery man, with a dozen red roses.

"Thank you," I said, taking the roses from him.

I put the flowers in a cobalt blue vase that Ray had owned, and set them on the counter. I stared at them as I opened the card.

To Hel,

Thank you for the good times you've already shown me, and the good times to come.

XOXO,
Raphael

My heart felt light as a feather, and I couldn't stop smiling. I was still smiling when Raphael came home half an hour later.

I heard his vehicle pulling into my driveway and met him at the door. He smiled when he saw me standing in the doorway, and grabbed his bags from the backseat.

His hair was shining in the sun, tempting me to run my fingers through its darkness, and I noticed his skin was darker after spending a few days working with me. He was still dressed in black, and against his silver Jeep, the whole scene had a kind of dangerous look.

Raphael's eyes locked with mine as he walked toward me. Everything else in the world faded as I stared back into those beautiful eyes.

I kissed him before he made it inside, before he could set his bags down. I kissed him with my whole body pressed against him until he moaned.

He pulled back enough to say, "So, I guess you got the flowers."

I pulled on his shirt to come on inside the house, and then led him over to the couch. He sat down and I stood in front of him, looking down and admiring the beautiful man looking up at me. I knew what I wanted to do, but it was something I had never been comfortable doing. What the hell, just do it… That was the phrase, right? Although, I'm pretty sure this was not what the company had in mind.

I knelt down in front of him and felt my face flush as I unzipped his pants. I kissed and gently bit at his stomach until his breath became more shallow, and I could feel him growing harder against my cheek. I moved his underwear out of my way and stroked the length of him, now more nervous than ever.

Raphael, once more seeming to read my mind, said, "You don't have to do anything you don't want to."

I smiled up at him; it must have been difficult to say that in his current situation. "I want to. I just haven't done this a lot, and I wasn't taking into account your size. If something doesn't feel good to you, just tell me."

He nodded and closed his eyes with a sharp breath as I licked and sucked him. He held my hair for me so he could see my face, but was careful to never pull it or push my head down.

My jaw ached and my gag reflex almost failed me once, but the little sounds Raphael made and the way he was looking at me, I'd keep doing this all day. Thankfully it didn't take that long.

After he finished, he pulled me to him and kissed me.

"Some guys don't like to kiss after that," I said.

"They're stupid, it's my body. If I won't kiss you after you've had your mouth there, it would be pretty sad for me to let you do it."

He kissed me again, and moved so I was lying on top of him on the couch. I nuzzled my face into his hair and we took a quick cat nap.

The ringing phone woke me up; it was Mr. Atkins, from the funeral home in town.

"Helena, we need a plot dug for Mrs. Mckinney's husband Joseph. He passed this morning."

It was always odd when they told me who it was. Normally they just told me the plot number and when they needed it; a name meant the person was pretty well known in town. The Mckinney's had been around forever. They were good people, and everyone knew Joseph had been battling lung cancer for a while now.

"Got it. I'll have it done by tomorrow evening," I said.

I walked back over to the couch where Raphael was lying. I leaned over and kissed him on the cheek. "I need to go work for a few hours," I said.

He opened his eyes, still heavy with sleep. "Want some help?"

"That's ok. You can stay in and rest, I'm not doing it all at once." I ran my fingers through his silken hair again and kissed his lips.

He nodded. "I'll make something for dinner."

"Sounds great," I said. I went into the bedroom and changed into digging clothes. I wanted to get this done so that tomorrow maybe Raphael and I could go into the city and I could shop for our trip.

Outside, the sky was softening into twilight. The day had passed more quickly than I thought it should have. I wanted to be curled up back on the couch with Raphael, but my muscles were stiff from inactivity and I knew that digging would help.

A breeze blew through the graveyard and chill bumps ran across my skin… strange. My first thought was maybe another summer storm was about the blow through. I looked around and none of the tree leaves were turned up, like they do when rain is coming; there were no dark clouds in the distance. It was just the violet gray of evening, but the cemetery was unsettling; the air was electric, almost threatening.

I didn't like being nervous out here, and my mind desperately searched for a reason I felt that way. I couldn't recall ever being scared in my cemetery: I knew this land and the people buried in it. I remembered the grave with the bracelet… was it related to that?

I walked by the grave; the outline of salt was still somewhat visible. I felt nothing from the grave, and nothing in the cemetery looked out of place.

I walked back over to plot where I was supposed to be digging, and thought about just going back to the cabin and starting again in the morning. But no, tomorrow I wanted to go shopping. I needed to get done as much as possible tonight.

The hair on the back of my neck stood up as if an icy breath had touched me. Another glance around the cemetery showed me why I was feeling uneasy: I was being watched.

In the tree line, there was a man standing, watching me. He wore faded jeans and a light blue polo shirt. My stomach twisted and rolled, I gripped the shovel tightly and fought the instinct telling me to run. He could be anyone—he wasn't necessarily dangerous. I put up my hand and waved to let him know I saw him.

The man walked towards me, and it was hard to

stand my ground. I couldn't understand where this fear was coming from. I dug at the plot just to so I could be moving. He had to walk a far distance, and it startled me when I heard him say, "Hello."

I was shocked at how quietly and quickly the man had moved, and when I looked up to see his face, I was only slightly relieved to see it was someone I already knew. It was my ex-boyfriend from college, the creepy one.

I forced a smile. "Hi, Brandon, I didn't know that was you." I swallowed hard and tried to ask myself why he would be out here watching me. Our breakup wasn't smooth, but it could have been a lot worse.

"Hello, Helena. How have you been?" His face showed nothing, just a talking body and a neutral voice.

"Good. Yourself? What brings you out here?" I asked. I resumed my digging—standing still was too uncomfortable, and I didn't want him to see that he was making me nervous.

"I've been well. I come out here sometimes and wander around," he said, and put his hands in his pockets.

I wondered if he was about to pull out a gun or knife. "Really? I haven't seen you out here," I said, my heart thudding just a little harder, prepping me to run if I needed to.

"I know. I've seen you, though." He watched for my reaction and pushed his large glasses up on his greasy face. His eyes were small even through the thick lenses, and his complexion showed a definite lack of care. He had gone downhill since our college days, and even then he wasn't exactly a catch. But I was willing to bet he was still scary smart, which is what had attracted me to him in the first place. It was the scary part that made me break up with him.

"Yeah, I'm usually lost in my own little world out here working. I don't always see everyone who comes by." That was the best I could do at not sounding freaked out. Oh, how I wished Raphael would walk out here; I'd settle for anybody showing up right now.

"I usually keep to edge of the woods so I can watch you work." His expression was still blank.

This time I had no words; I knew my face paled as I looked at him. I swallowed.

"You never let me dig with you, Hel. What's special about him?" Brandon was shifting his weight from side to side now. He was getting agitated.

He had seen Raphael working with me. He had stood in the shadows and watched us work together— I'd had no clue. I felt so ill.

"You wanted to have sex in a grave and see the bodies. He just wanted to help me get my work done. If you want to help me dig now, I can go get you a shovel." *Please let that work, please let that work.*

"Whose grave is this going to be?" he asked nodding towards the plot.

"Joseph Mckinney," I answered.

I saw rage bubble up from somewhere deep inside. It filled his eyes, and his hands clenched at his sides.

"My grandfather! You want me to help you dig a grave for my own grandfather?" he wailed.

He paced in small circles, clenching and relaxing his fists. He was mumbling to himself, and I heard something about "that sick bitch" that I could only assume was me.

"I'm sorry, Brandon. I forgot he was your grandfather. I'm sure I'll have another to dig in a day or two. I can let you know," I mumbled, trying not to raise my voice at all. "I could probably even pay you to help me some if you're really interested." I swam through the fear in my brain, looking for more things to say that might distract him. "So, where are you working these days?"

He looked at me with an expression of absolute disgust, ignoring all of my ramblings.

"I should make you dig your own grave, then I could get everything I wanted from you."

My brain heard what he said, but it refused to process all the vile possibilities he could be insinuating. Every muscle in my body wanted to run, but my feet refused to move.

"That's a good idea, come to think of it," he said, and walked in closer to me.

I had the shovel in my hand, but I didn't want to strike first. I was still hoping he was just being creepy, and this wouldn't end in violence on either part. But my gut was telling me it wouldn't be that easy.

He circled around me, looking me up and down. "I could fuck you and kill you and leave you in a grave you dug yourself. Or I could kill you, then fuck you, so you couldn't put up a fight; leave you for your pretty little boyfriend to find."

I wanted to vomit, but I fought it, instead I gripped the shovel and brought it down as hard as I could on his foot. It didn't connect as hard as I had hoped. I wanted it to chop half of his foot off. Instead, it just made him angrier.

"Bitch!" he spat at me as he grabbed my ponytail and painfully yanked my neck backwards.

I cried out, then screamed, "Let go of me!"

I swung the shovel and tried to connect with any part of his body, it was too long for me to get a good angle while he was this close. I didn't want to drop my weapon, but just maybe if I did I could use that other hand to scratch and claw my way out his grasp. I saw the mattock on the ground; the sharp end with the pick could definitely slow him down, or stop him for good. That was the weapon I needed.

I dropped the shovel and grabbed his arm, digging my nails into his flesh and pulling at his arm hair. I screamed and fought, and when he brought his hand up to cover my mouth, I bit him until I tasted blood, and ripped off a piece of skin with my teeth. I spat the flesh out, and tried not to think about the taste that was lingering in my mouth.

He howled and shoved me away from him hard before gripping his injured hand.

This was my chance to get away. I tried to gain my footing to run, but it was no use: I tripped from the force of his push, and as my body went down, I felt my head smash against the hard, sharp edge of a gravestone. I felt the hit echo throughout my head, and for a moment I couldn't move. I fought to stay conscious, to get away, but I could only see out of one eye now, and everything was blurred.

I could try to make it to the cabin, back across the cemetery, back to Raphael where he could call 911; or I could go towards the road and hope someone saw me and took me to get help. I felt blood pouring down the side of my face and neck; the collar of my shirt was already soaked and sticky, and I didn't know how much I could afford to lose. My head was burning with pain and my eyes were stinging with sweat and blood, plus I was sure I had a concussion.

I needed help fast. I went towards the cabin to warn Raphael; I couldn't see Brandon, but I didn't hear him anymore. Maybe he had gotten scared and run. I knew my wounds were severe, but I didn't think they were lethal just yet.

The sky was nearly dark now, and I was trying to navigate myself towards the cabin without tripping over every headstone along the way. My legs were scraped from the stones I didn't see, and I felt like I wasn't doing much better than I would crawling. I saw the porch light and kept what little sight I had focused. I could make it.

Suddenly, I was brought to the ground by a force like a train hitting me. Sharp, searing, otherworldly pain ran through me like lightning. I wanted to scream but whatever had hit me knocked the air out of my lungs—or had it punctured a lung? I felt the presence of someone standing over me and knew it had to be Brandon; then I remembered the mattock. The bastard had used it on me. I wanted to curse at him, to threaten his life, but I had no air—just pain… and then it all stopped.

In a moment of clarity, I realized I was on pavement: I had been going the wrong direction all along, following the glow of a street lamp instead of the cabin's porch light. Darkness was closing in on me; I tried so hard to fight it—to hang onto any bit of light and life. It was just all too much, and the darkness was so very heavy. But I was on the road, and that filled me with relief. *Good*, I thought, *Raphael won't be the one to find my body.*

CHAPTER SIX

People aren't wrong about the bright
light. That's the first thing I saw when I woke up, if
you can call it that: waking up.

"Hey," a gruff voice shouted, and someone shook
my arm like they were waking me up from a nap.

I raised my arm against the agonizing light, and the
person turned it away from my eyes. The man offered
me a hand to sit up. His hand was huge compared to
mine, and mine weren't exceptionally small.

I sat up and realized I was covered in dirt; everything
around me was dark except for what the brilliant
flashlight shined on. I saw the light reflect off of what
could only be a shovel. The evening's events came
into focus: Brandon, the graveyard. Had he thought
he killed me and tried to bury me?

"Did you dig me up?" I asked.

"I did," the gruff voice said again.

I couldn't see the man's face, but from the shadows
he cast, he was tall, and had shoulders as wide as a
doorway.

"I need to get to a hospital. I have a bad head injury,"
I said. But as I touched the side of my head, I didn't

feel a cut, or the stickiness of drying blood. I looked at the man, clearly confused.

Another voice, another man I couldn't see, said something from in the darkness. The man with me answered, "Yeah, it always sucks when they don't know."

I knew what he wanted to tell me, but I didn't want to hear it. Tears were already streaming down my face faster than I had ever known them to fall. All I could picture was Raphael's beautiful face, and all I could feel was my heart breaking so hard that it might have killed me, if I wasn't already dead.

"Ah hell, she's crying," the gruff man said. "Can you come get her? She's got to get assigned."

I heard the other man walking up. "Yeah, I'll take her if you'll wake my next three." His voice was higher, and he had an accent I recognized.

The gruff man made a noise that sounded like "yeah," and walked off.

The other man walked over to where I sat in the dirt and kneeled down next to me. He was skinny and lanky; he was missing a few teeth and had a few poorly done tattoos, but he patted my shoulder with empathy.

"It'll be ok honey. I know it's quite a shock. I need you to come with me though, so they can get you assigned." His voice was much more gentle than the big man's.

"Assigned?" I croaked out through my sobs. "Am I in heaven or hell?" Looking around as my vision cleared, it certainly didn't seem like heaven, and although it didn't look like a happy place, it didn't seem bad enough to be hell.

"You're kind of in an in-between place. You must not have been religious in life or had any set belief systems. When that happens and you die, you come here. You'll be assigned living quarters and a job," he explained.

"Do I have to stay here forever?" I looked around; it didn't seem like much, from what I could tell.

"You can, or you can choose a religion or reincarnation, but you'll have to work the rest of your time off first."

"What do you mean, work off the rest of my time?"

"We all sign contracts in spirit, before being born, that we'll serve so many years on earth. An early death equals time owed," he said as we walked. "You'll get one of these to keep track of everything," he held up his arm showing me a small black watch on his wrist.

"Even if you're murdered?" I asked.

"If you're murdered and don't have set beliefs. There are all kinds of bylaws and stuff." He shrugged. "Even in death, you can't get away from politics."

"So if I'd been a Christian, I could be in Heaven right now?" I asked.

"Yep."

"That blows." I realized I wasn't crying anymore, and somehow that caused a stabbing pain in my heart.

"It's not all bad here. As long as you do your job, you can do pretty much whatever you want," he said.

As we walked, the scenery changed from flat dirt covered lands, to sidewalks that ran through what looked like an old, tired city.

A man with paper white skin and curly long red hair stepped out from the shadows of a building. His eyes had no white, but looked as though they could have been cut from emeralds. His nose and cheek bones were sharp.

"Hello, lovely new girl," the strange looking man said.

"Not right now, Boude. She's on her way to be assigned," said the man with me. I hadn't realized I'd stopped walking and was staring at the pale man with the flaming hair.

My guy tugged on my shirt and we continued.

"Who was that? What was he?"

"That's Boude; he's a vampire. Best stay away from them."

"Vampire? What!" I froze. I admit, I had never given much thought to vampires before. I recalled watching Lost Boys with Raphael and almost had to laugh, but not in the 'haha' kind of way—more like the 'oh shit' kind of way.

My scrawny guide just glanced at me and motioned to keep walking. "You'll learn it all, eventually," he said.

I looked around my surroundings again. There was light, but no sun; it felt overcast, but there were no clouds. And the sky—it was just… gray.

We rounded a corner, and there was a line of people waiting outside a rather plain brown building. I found my guide showing me where to take my place, and estimated being number thirty, at best.

"OK," he said, "you just wait here, and when you get in there, answer all the questions they have. Make sure you don't lie: they already know the answers to most of the questions they ask. They're usually pretty nice, though; you'll be fine."

"Are you leaving me here?" I realized I still didn't

know his name. I didn't know him, but he was the only person I'd really met so far. I didn't want to be alone.

"I have to get back to work." He smiled his gap-tooth smile.

"What's your name?" I asked.

"Billy," he said, and held his hand out.

I shook his hand and said, "Thank you, Billy."

"You're welcome. See you around."

And with that, I was by myself again. I was alone in a line of people—dead people—waiting to be told what to do next. I was heartbroken and scared. Death was already worse than I could have imagined.

No one in the line tried to talk to me, and I was grateful. Whether I was simply lost in thought, or these people were efficient, the line moved faster than I would have expected. Before I knew it, it was my turn.

The doors were elaborate for the plain looking building. They were ornately carved, and appeared to be painted gold, with some type of pearl-like inlay. From far away they looked impressive, but up-close they looked cheap. I wondered if they were some sad replica of heaven's gates. It seemed mocking to me, but maybe it was intended as a comfort or flattery.

"Helena Pierce."

I heard my name called from a room to the left. I poked my head in and saw a small woman sitting behind a large mahogany desk.

"Yes, ma'am," I answered.

"Come in and have a seat please, Ms. Pierce." Her hair was brown, and curled close to her head. Silver glasses sat on her nose, attached to a chain that hung down around her neck.

I sat down in one of the chairs in front of her.

"I see you were murdered. Being here must be a surprise for you." Her voice was monotone and nasal. "Well, I think you'll find most people get along here pretty well. It looks like you have sixty-five years to work off here: that would have been when you were supposed to die." The lady was scribbling something down in a book.

Sixty-five years here sounded terrifying. I was originally supposed to die at eighty-seven; that would have been nice.

"Is there any way to lessen that?" I asked.

The woman scribbled some more and nodded. "Well, a lot of it depends on the job you take: more labor-intensive work takes off more time, choosing a religion or reincarnation takes some, but you still have to work off the time you owe."

"Do you assign me a job or can I choose?" I asked.

"Either way." The woman actually smiled at me.

"Which job shaves off the most hours?"

"Reaping," she said.

I immediately pictured a scythe and a long black cloak following people around when it was 'their time,' but had the sense to ask, "What is that?"

"The person who woke you up was a reaper. You work in the fields, so to speak; you would dig up the deceased and send them here to get assigned, or if their souls are spoken for, you send them on their way. It is a labor-intensive job," she told me. "But, being a gravedigger in life, you might find it appealing."

"How many hours will that earn me?" I asked.

"You work when you want, but realize you're only

working off time when you *are* working. You owe 569,400 hours, reaping takes off five hours for every hour of work."

I couldn't do the math in my head, but I knew that was still a lot of time.

"Of course, you don't have to eat or sleep here, but most people still choose to. There are restaurants and such comforts. You will be assigned lodging near your work; we don't have many reapers, so you should have a place all to yourself. You'll check in with me every five hundred hours. Any questions?"

"Is there any way to communicate with the living?" I couldn't stop myself from asking.

She gave me a pitying look and sighed. "Not unless you pay a pretty hefty price. You can go back as a ghost, but interaction is limited. Also, ghosts tend to get so focused on being back in that world that they can't get back to the afterlife: they get trapped and confused. If vampirism seems appealing, remember: they give up their souls to be able to interact with the living. You would have to consume living blood to walk among them, and should you ever be killed, your soul would cease to exist forever."

Tears filled my eyes once more. "Those are my only options?" I asked.

She smiled gently. "Now and then the sun shines here, and when it does, the veil between worlds is thin. You can go to the fountain in the center of the city, look in, and see those that you miss."

It wasn't much, but I'd take it. "Thank you," I said.

She handed me a map of this place, and circled where I was and how to get back to the fields. She also handed me a small black watch like the one that Billy had shown me.

"Wear this: it will keep track of the hours you work. Good luck to you," she said, and sent me out the door.

I was on my own for the time being. I walked around the gray city of the afterlife as I would any other city: by keeping my eyes forward and acting like I knew what I was doing.

I had no idea if people here could hurt me, or if anyone was dangerous. Out of curiosity I pinched myself as hard as I could. It did hurt, and it left a little red mark that ached after I let go. Well, that answered one question.

There were shops and stores with clothing. I thought about going in, but had no idea how I would pay. What kind of money was there here, anyway?

Then I smelled a scent that brought me comfort and sadness all at the same time: coffee.

A little shop with a brown awning was where the aroma was coming from. I peeked in and saw people sitting at tables sipping out of various cups. If I hadn't known any better, I could have been at any living coffee shop.

I wandered in and looked around, trying not to be too obvious or get in anyone's way.

"Can I help you?" the barista asked. She was younger than me, with black hair that I didn't think was her natural color, and several piercings. The whole situation raised a lot of questions, but I didn't need to ask just yet.

"I, uhh, I was just looking." I kept watching, hoping someone would place an order so I could see how they paid.

"What do you like?" A voice asked from behind me, the sound ran across my skin like velvet.

Startled, I turned to see the red-haired vampire, standing close enough that if I leaned back half an inch we'd be touching.

"Hi," I squeaked out—my heart was pounding. How did that work, being dead? I put my hand over my chest.

The vampire smiled at me with closed lips. "It's the memory of your heart racing that you feel. There's no need to fear me."

He looked down into my eyes. It was so unsettling to look at eyes that didn't look like eyes. I stared into the green abyss and saw my reflection, pitiful-looking, and lonely—dead.

He stared longer, and I found myself feeling calmer. "What kind of coffee do you want?"

"Just black, please," I said.

As he turned away to order for me, I saw there was no exchange of money. He handed me the cup and saw my perplexed expression. "We don't use money here. Sometimes we trade, but mostly we have access to everything we need. So if you need something, just ask."

"Thank you," I said, looking into his eyes. It still unnerved me that I couldn't tell what he was focused on. Maybe one day I'd ask him how that worked.

I held my hand out to him, "We haven't officially been introduced. I'm Helena. Call me Hel."

He took my hand and laid a soft kiss on the back

of my fingers. "It's a pleasure, Ms. Hel. My name is Boudewijn, but you may call me Boude." Then he asked, "Have you been assigned yet?"

"Yes, I'm a reaper," I said.

His eyes seemed to widen at that.

"Such a taxing job for a pretty one." His long white fingers curled in front of his lips as if he were trying to hide his surprise.

"I was a gravedigger in life. I don't mind work," I told him. "I really should be off. I have to get to the fields and see where I'll be living." I was still feeling out of sorts and anxious.

He stepped aside without hesitation. "Good luck on adjusting to your new surroundings. If you need anything... please ask."

I smiled at him and waved goodbye as I went on my way. First official meeting with a vampire was in the books, and it wasn't so bad.

I followed the map out of the city, and soon found myself standing at the edge of barren land. There was nothing but dark brown, rich dirt as far as I could see. As I walked through the land, I looked down at the dirt and saw there were small silver name tags marking the people waiting to be brought up.

This wasn't anything like the graveyards at home. There was no lush green grass, no trees, no angel statues to watch over us. It was dull, lonely, and not at all what I wanted forever to look like.

The gray of the horizon and brown of the dirt was all I could see, and I had already been walking for what seemed like miles. Where the hell was I supposed to live?

Finally, I saw someone digging out in the distance.

Another reaper, perhaps? He should know what I need to do.

It took longer to walk to the person in the distance than I anticipated. But finally, I got there, and was met with, "Why are you back?"

I recognized the man as the one who had dug me up: the big, tough guy, who was unhappy that I had cried.

"I'm assigned as a reaper," I said. "Can you please tell me where the living quarters are?"

He rolled his eyes and sighed. "I swear, what were they thinking, making you a reaper?"

It made me mad that I would still have to deal with such pig-headed thinking even after death. I could have argued—I wanted to—but I shrugged. "Living quarters?" I repeated.

He rubbed his beard and made a 'follow me' motion over his shoulder as he started walking. I followed him through more rows of the dead and down a new path I hadn't seen. Sure enough, there they were: plain little brown houses, all lined up next to one another.

"Number six is empty. You can take it," he said.

"Thanks," I said, and stuck out my hand to him. "I'm Helena, Hel for short."

He eyed my hand suspiciously. "Soren."

I picked up his hand from his side and shook it. "Nice to meet you, Soren."

A smile passed through his eyes but he didn't let it cross his lips. For a moment I thought maybe he could be attractive, but he seemed happier being feared.

Soren dug around in his pockets for a moment and fished out a rectangular silver key with the number six engraved on the side. He handed me the key and said,

"See you around."

I walked up to the plain brown door of the plain brown house, and sighed. I could feel the emotions welling back up inside of me. I was going to cry again, and it was going to be bad. Once more I pushed everything back down and told myself to look at my new living quarters first; then I could have my breakdown.

I turned the key and turned the knob and walked inside.

The layout was simple, loft style: a full-sized bed against the wall, a table with two chairs, and a small kitchen, complete with a plate and cup. I opened a door at the far end of the house and found a bathroom. I appreciated seeing the shower immediately, but had questions about the toilet. I mean, I'm dead—is this still relevant?

I sat on the bed and looked around the house. I had nothing to make it mine yet, but maybe that was okay. My heart wasn't here—why should I try to make it cozy? I closed my eyes and saw Raphael's face. I wondered how he was, how much I had hurt him by leaving in such an awful way? I seethed with anger towards the man who had killed me. How dare he take away everything that I loved! I cried, and I cried, but it didn't help. The more I cried, the more emotions welled up inside of me. Pain filled my being—real physical pain, as if I was on fire from the inside. I screamed over and over, trying to release even an ounce.

Suddenly there were arms around me, picking me up off of the floor. I hadn't even realized I had moved from the bed. I could distantly hear voices, but they were muffled by my screams and sobs.

I was on my feet, and now, I was facing Soren. He was shaking me hard by my shoulders.

"Stop screaming!" he shouted in my face.

His huge hands wrapped completely around my arms, and I was having to look up to see his eyes. He was strong, and serious, and very blonde, I noticed, right down to his beard.

I stopped screaming, but the tears still streamed down my face. I was broken.

"We could hear you screaming a mile away, literally," he said. "Get outside and get to work. Make this your new normal; don't dwell on where you are, because there isn't a damn thing you can do about it."

He stared down into my eyes and I saw a trace of empathy, then he hardened himself and let me go.

It was only after he was out the door that I turned and saw the skinny guy that had taken me to get assigned, Billy.

"Don't hold it against him. Being mean and tough is the way Soren gets through all of this. He's a good guy.

"You OK for me to leave you now?" he asked.

I nodded and forced a smile. "I'm sorry I caused such a scene." I felt my face turn a little red.

"No worries, first day is the worst. But Soren is right: the more you can work and get settled, it'll help. If you need anything just holler."

I waved and watched as Billy went out the door. I really was embarrassed at myself for throwing such a fit, even if it was warranted. I was tougher than this; I knew that death was part of life, I was just on the other side of it this time. I took a deep breath and let it out slowly.

I washed my face, and with nothing else to do, I went outside to do what I do best: dig.

CHAPTER SEVEN

Outside near the houses I found a utility building that contained all the tools I was used to. I grabbed a pair of gloves and the things I needed, and set off to find Billy or someone to show me what to do. I wasn't too keen on Soren teaching me, since he wasn't the friendliest, but I needed to get started.

I walked through row after row of people in the ground. It reminded me of walking through a garden and trying not to step on the plants. I had walked through rows of people before in cemeteries, but this felt so different. Maybe it was because these people were waiting to wake up and be pulled *from* the dirt, instead of having been placed *in* it to sleep peacefully.

I heard the ting of a shovel and the soft fall of dirt, and turned to see Billy and Soren working down one of the rows. They were so close I don't know how I could have missed them.

"Hey," I shouted at them, and set down my shovel. "I'm ready to work."

Billy smiled his lacking smile at me, and Soren waved me over with a less than enthusiastic motion.

"Digging is no easy task," the big man told me. His

hands around the handle of the shovel made it look tiny. "Each spot you can dig has a small name tag. None of us pay attention to them other than to know there's someone in that spot."

Billy chimed in, "Now and then, someone can't remember who they are, and keep asking their name. It helps with that too."

I nodded.

Soren went on, "They're only a few feet down, and not in coffins or anything, so don't go too fast, and feel for things below the soil before you dig too hard, and they wake up with a shovel in them."

I bit my lip, trying to resist asking questions about how he knew this, and trying to stifle a chuckle. Waking up dead would definitely be worse with a shovel through your stomach.

"Once you can see them, you shine your light in their face. If their soul is spoken for, they'll disappear, and you fill in the hole. If they come to, you lead them to get assigned, come back, and fill in your hole. Clear enough?"

"Clear," I said.

I was glad I had picked up a flashlight out of the utility room. "Can I start near you guys, in case I have questions?"

"Yep, but don't expect us to do your work for you when you get tired," Soren snorted.

"Understood," I said. *Big, Viking, Asshole.*

I found a name tag, and tried not to pay attention to the name. I didn't want to know the people I was digging up, I just wanted to dig up a lot of them. I placed my shovel down in the dirt, and to my amazement, it slid right in. I scooped up the loose rich earth and tossed it to the side, followed by another, and another. I didn't need a mattock, and I didn't have to jump on the shovel to get it to budge. I couldn't feel any big rocks under the earth clanging against the shovel in protest. It was only earth—earth and people.

It was no time before I felt the shovel touch something softer than the earth. The hole I had dug was only about two-and-a-half feet down, but I moved away the dirt in a more gentle sweeping motion, rather than digging.

Soon, I had uncovered an older woman with white hair curled close to her head. She looked peaceful in her royal blue jacket and skirt. Tied around her neck was a white scarf with little pink roses that matched her lipstick.

I got out my flashlight and had a moment of panic. What if she didn't disappear? What if she woke up in hysterics, like I had? Could I really deal with that right now?

I saw Soren eyeing me, and knew I needed to keep moving before he said something insulting again. So, I took out my flashlight and clicked it on, shining like a sun in the little woman's face.

The old woman's eyes flew open, and her mouth seemed to part in shock as what looked like electricity passed through her body—then she was gone. I was left staring at an empty hole.

"Good job," Billy said.

I smiled at him, quite pleased with myself.

I dug up three more people within the hour, all of whose souls were claimed. The digging was easy, and I didn't seem to get tired. Maybe I could work my time off even faster than I had hoped.

As I headed into my next hour of work, Billy seemed to watch me in amazement. He nudged Soren and said, "If she gets any faster, she'll be out digging you."

Soren grumbled, "I'm just glad she can carry her own weight around here."

I smiled and kept digging, glad to have earned maybe an ounce of respect. I dug for hours. I felt as fresh on hour six as I did when I first got started. My mind felt numb to things I didn't want to think about, and I'd do whatever it took to keep it that way.

"C'mon," Billy called, motioning me over.

"Where?" I replied, and wiped the sweat from my brow. Not six hours' worth of sweat, but it was interesting to know my body kind of worked the same here.

"We're going to call it a night. Get some food, rest a little," he said.

This place was so confusing. "Do we sleep?" I asked, puzzled.

"You can, but you don't have to. Breaks and rest are good though, otherwise you kinda become a zombie," he shrugged.

Having just met a vampire earlier, my mind immediately went to the brain-eating kind of monster. "Wait, what?" I asked.

"Not a cannibal-zombie, just mindless, going through the motions. It's easy to get stuck in working off your time and not take care of yourself. Just get a bite to eat and sit back a while," Soren said.

I didn't want to take care of myself or rest. I didn't want to think about the things I left behind. I would rather work and let my brain go to mush. I stared out into the bleakness of the sky and dirt.

Soren's warm hand on my wrist made me look down.

"Come on, Hel." His touch and voice were gentle for a change.

I looked down at his hand on me, and I appreciated the gentleness, but I shook my head no. "I need to keep digging. I can't stop to think," I said, and made my face as blank as I could.

Soren let go of my arm and nodded. In that moment I knew he understood. He understood the agony that was waiting in my mind—waiting to attack at the first sign of calmness, at the first sign of hope.

I worked, and worked, and worked. They sky never changed, even though the hours passed. I didn't keep track of how many hours or how many bodies.

Then, upon digging up a middle-aged man, for the first time in all of my hours, he didn't disappear.

The large man with a receding hairline and bright blue eyes seemed to know he was dead, so I was off the hook for that at least. But, he had to be taken to be assigned.

I found another reaper, one I hadn't met yet,and told him where I was going and that I'd get my things when I got back. The other reaper was a tall black man who just nodded and walked off. *OK, then.*

I tried talking to the man on our walk, but he remained quiet, just staring at the things around him in awe. I realized as we walked that the fields of the dead seemed to be in the outermost region of this place. There was no road past it; I wondered what was on the other side, and reminded myself to look at my map when I got back.

I left the man standing in line and turned to go back,

staring in the windows of the few little shops I passed. I wanted some new clothes, but couldn't seem to bring myself to go in and browse.

From the window I saw the shop owner turn to face me. His eyes were a glowing fiery amber, no white, no pupil. He was another vampire.

Not being able to resist, I walked in, said hello, and began looking around.

"Hello," said the vampire. "May I help you find anything?"

"Hi there. Thanks, but I'm just not sure what I'm looking for," I said.

"Perhaps something besides what you were buried in? Something to make you feel part of this world?" The vampire smiled without showing teeth.

I wondered if all vampires were so beautiful. His blonde hair fell around his face in a graceful sweep that most girls could never manage to achieve. He was tall, yet thin and delicate.

"Is it weird that I don't want to let go of this?" I asked, tugging at the flowered blouse I couldn't even remember owning.

"Darling, nothing is weird here." His long slim fingers gently tossed his hair back over his shoulder, and he winked an amber eye at me.

A giggle caught in my throat; I couldn't bring myself to let it out, but I smiled.

When he walked over to me from behind the counter, I saw he was wearing flowy, black bell-bottom pants, and a peasant style black shirt embroidered with gold beads that brought out the gold in his eyes.

"Love the outfit," I smiled.

"It's all in here," he said with a wave of his arm.

"I was looking for something more… me. Jeans, maybe—t-shirt?"

He shrugged. "Well you're cute enough to pull anything off."

"Thanks," I said as he led the way through the shop.

"How long have you been here, doll?" he asked as he held up a pair of jeans in front of my waist, and shook his head no, choosing another pair.

"Uhh, yesterday, this morning? I haven't really figured out time here," I admitted, and chose a black t-shirt hanging nearby on a rack.

"If you do figure it out, let me know. Things are what they are here, until they aren't." He finally selected a pair of dark wash jeans and handed them to me. "Here, go try these on."

I went behind the little curtain in the back and changed into my new clothes. They fit, and made me feel more like myself. I looked at the old jeans and shirt I had been buried in. It made me wonder: who chose that for me to spend eternity in? Practical, yes, but not very pretty. Not that it mattered, anyway.

"Do you like the clothes?" the vampire called.

"Yes, they work well," I answered.

"Great, you can just keep them on," he replied, and pulled back the curtain.

He looked me over and nodded. "Nice, but are you certain you don't want something more interesting?"

"I'm a reaper. I'm afraid anything more interesting wouldn't work out too well." I smiled.

He shrugged and wrinkled his brow. "Why are you a reaper?" He asked with obvious distaste.

"I was a gravedigger in life. I wanted to stick with what I know."

"I was a train engineer. I wanted to do nothing like what I did in life," he giggled.

I thanked him for the help and said goodbye, heading back to the field.

The sky still looked like a wet blanket had been spread across it, and the fields of dead under the ground still went on forever. I missed rain and sunshine, and most of all, wind. I couldn't register a temperature here, not in myself or my surroundings. I wasn't uncomfortable, but to not be able to "feel" hot or cold on my skin was inhuman.

I wanted to lie down and rest, so I went to my little box that I had been assigned. The inside was laid out so much like the home I had lived in, my heart ached and I swallowed down the tears. I wondered if pain got better in time here... Or would I always hurt this much?

Lying on the bed, I closed my eyes. Darkness pulled me in, and I felt like I was floating, then flying through space and time. Memories of Ray and my childhood danced before my eyes, then traveling and my college years. Raphael was suddenly there, introducing himself, kissing me, inside me, and I felt myself shudder. Then I saw myself die, so bloody and torn, dragging myself to the road and letting go.

I opened my eyes and gasped. I didn't want to remember any of that. I just wanted death to be peace and darkness—nothingness.

Something caught my eye just outside the window. Was that... sunshine? The golden rays were streaking down over the plain brown dirt like little strands of hope. I remembered what the lady had told me about being able to see the living when the sun shines here. I jumped up and was out the door faster than I had ever moved in my life.

I ran through the fields towards the city, ignoring every person I saw. I had to get to the fountain. I tried to remember where I had seen the fountain, but it was a blur in my head from the excitement I was feeling.

I spotted a man walking the opposite way and paused just long enough to ask him, "Excuse me, sir, where is the fountain in town?"

His smile was kind, but he shook his head. "It's two streets down. Don't look though, it's harder than you think."

I thanked him and ran on, not even considering turning back. This was my chance to see Raphael.

I could barely see the fountain as I approached, even though it was huge. People were everywhere, squeezed in on top of one another, to get a glimpse of the people they had left behind. I tried to squeeze my way in too. It didn't matter if I had to sit on a stranger's lap to see, even for a second.

A woman at the edge of the fountain turned to me as she dried her tears. "Here, you can take my spot. I was only checking on my son."

"Thank you," I laid my hand on her shoulder and slid into her spot as she fought her way out.

I could see the fountain more clearly now. The water flowed down from the top, filling what looked like little silver bowls all the way down, each bowl overflowing into the next one. I looked down into the bowl in front of me and saw nothing. I glanced around and saw people putting a finger into the water, so I tried that.

The moment my skin touched the water, I saw it—like a movie playing in front of me. I saw my cabin, empty of my things. I saw my graveyard, heavy machinery digging a grave. It hurt.

Instead, I thought about Raphael. Then, I saw him too. He was in his Jeep, sitting somewhere that I knew had to be out west. He was parked on a mountain, looking out at tall red rocks and a beautiful sunset. He looked peaceful, and I was thankful.

He took out his phone, opened the lock screen and stared down at the picture on the background: it was me. Raphael had taken a candid picture of me sitting in the floor of my living room after our first official date. My hair was down and I was smiling.

He touched the picture and his breath came out harsh and long. Then he scrolled through other pictures in his phone until he found one of a sunset like the one in front of him, and changed the background.

I bit my lip, fighting back tears for more reasons than I could begin to count. He was so beautiful, and his eyes were so full of sadness—sadness I only ever wanted to fix, but instead ended up making so much worse.

I pulled myself up from the fountain, and numbly turned to go back to the field. My feet carried me forward, but my brain was turned off. I wasn't thinking about Raphael; I wasn't thinking about digging graves. I couldn't feel anything. I pulled up every shield I could muster and forced myself to feel nothing.

I kept waiting for the acres of brown and dead to

come up in the distance, but everywhere I looked there were only gray buildings and gray sidewalk. It didn't take a genius to figure out I had gotten myself turned around. *Damn.*

Things felt as though they were closing in around me, and the wall of numbness I had faked was slipping. I had nowhere to go that felt safe, nowhere that held even an ounce of comfort.

Movement caught my eye down one of the shadowed alleys. I walked towards it, hoping to find someone to ask which direction I needed to be going. As I made my way into the shadows, I seemed to still be all alone, but it felt… different.

There was no sound, and from what I could see there was no one in the alley with me. I looked up as I walked, silently remarking on the Gothic architecture towering above me. The buildings had turned from gray to black, and seemed to be close enough to touch at their peaks, creating an archway to walk beneath. That was why it was so dark.

I felt as though I was walking into an entirely different world. The sidewalk seemed to narrow, and once again I found myself feeling claustrophobic. I stopped and looked back, only to see I had walked so far into the darkness here that I couldn't see the road I had started on.

A figure stepped out of the shadows beside me, and I screamed. He didn't react. I could tell he was a vampire, but something about him was different from the others I had met. The other vampires I'd seen were beautiful, entrancing. This one had stringy white hair that hung in clumps against his visible scalp; paper-thin, chalky skin that I could see the blue and red veins beneath. The eyes weren't lovely like the other vampires I had seen, just endless pools of cold blackness.

He tilted his head at unnatural angles trying to figure me out, like a dog that hears a strange noise, then he stepped in closer and smelled my hair.

"Freshly dead," he hissed, and smiled showing fangs, yellow and black with rot.

I choked back another scream, and backed slowly away from the vampire. Something was very wrong here.

His eyes were on mine, and when I thought I could turn to run, he grabbed me by the wrist and pulled it up to his mouth.

This time I did scream, I screamed and kicked and tried to pull at his hair. None of my flailing seemed to bother him in the slightest; he opened his mouth to bite, and I closed my eyes.

"She's a friend, Rasputin." I recognized the voice as Boude.

The pathetic vampire in front of me dropped my arm, and then did what I can only describe as "scampered" back into the shadows.

I turned around to see Boude standing behind me; he practically glowed, with his red curls and gold waistcoat. His green eyes sparkled at me and he smiled, careful not to show fangs.

I ran to him and he pulled me into his arms. A small sob escaped my lips as I buried my face in his hair.

"There, there," he comforted as he petted my hair. "You're safe. He won't bother you again."

"I thought vampires couldn't drink from us if we're already dead," I said between heaves.

"Shouldn't… it doesn't truly sustain us, which is why Rasputin looks the way he does. Over time, our brains turn to mush on dead blood, as well, so it can drive us mad." Boude squeezed me to him a little tighter as my sobs turned to sniffles.

"Is that the 'real' Rasputin?" I asked, recalling the history stories.

"No one is really certain. He seems to think so, but he's been drinking dead blood for quite some time now. This is the Vampire's Quarter, not very safe for you. Most of us are harmless, but still, what were you doing here?"

"I went to the fountain to look, then I was distraught trying to find my way back to the fields, and got turned around." I dropped my head so that my forehead was against his chest, he smelled like spices, like incense, and underneath, a very faint scent of pennies.

Boude raised my chin up to look at him. I would never get used to looking a vampire in the eyes. It was too confusing with no pupils.

"Sweet little, Hel. That fountain brings much more sorrow than relief. You have to move on." He paused. "The one you miss has, hasn't he?"

I bit my lip to hold back a tear, but it didn't work. The hot, wet drop rolled down my face, and Boude wiped it away, cupping the side of my face in his hand. His skin was warmer and softer than I had expected. I closed my eyes and sighed. I felt his other arm tighten around my back, and then his lips were on mine, oh so softly. I tensed and pulled back. I opened my eyes only to be staring right into the shining emerald gems that were his.

He blushed, which I didn't know was possible, and

said, "Forgive me. I just wanted to comfort you. I—"

I stopped his words with my mouth back on his. This kiss was longer, but still gentle and soft.

He broke the kiss this time and searched my face. Apparently, he liked what he saw because he smiled. "May I walk you back to the fields?"

"Yes, please."

Arm in arm, we walked back through the gray city to the brown fields, and as long as I was touching him, my mind was peaceful. I wondered if it was some kind of vampire magic, but didn't care.

As we approached the fields I saw Soren and Billy digging nearby. A look of disgust crossed Soren's face.

"What are you doing here, vampire?" Soren spat the last word.

"The lady found herself in a less than ideal situation. She asked me to help her find her way back," Boude replied.

Soren made some kind of snorting sound. "Well, be on your way soon."

I was angry. "He's my friend, and he can stay as long as I say." My voice was shaky, but biting.

Soren shook his head in disapproval, but went back to digging. Billy said nothing; he just watched, then started digging again.

As we walked on toward the housing, I told Boude I was sorry for Soren's behavior.

"Many people don't like vampires. They think it's evil or weak that we give up our souls to walk among the living for as long as we choose," Boude shrugged.

"I can understand making that choice. I don't think it's evil or weak," I said.

"Don't tell me you are considering it yourself?" the

vampire inquired with a look I perceived as eagerness.

I shrugged. "I don't know." We stopped walking in front of my little place. "I kind of think I should keep my soul."

"Well I will support you with any choice you make. Thank you for letting me walk you home." He kissed my hand and turned to leave.

"Thanks again for saving me."

"Anytime," he said, and gave a small bow.

I walked up to my door, and as I turned the knob I was struck by the evening's events, and the most overwhelming feeling of loneliness. It was such a deep, heart crushing feeling that I simply couldn't bear it. I turned around and called out to the vampire walking away from me.

"Boude."

He turned, an inquisitive look on his face, and walked back towards me.

I went to him and tangled my fingers in his hair as I kissed him, long and deep, before pulling back to say, "I don't think I can stand being alone. Will you stay with me?"

Wordlessly, he scooped me up and carried me into the house, gently kicking the door closed behind him. He laid me down on the bed and kissed me. I watched as he undressed me, gently caressing my skin with touches and kisses.

I helped him out of his waistcoat and shirt, and ran my fingers along his smooth skin. Images of Raphael filled my mind: my nights with him, the care he took with my body, and the immense desire I had for him. Boude was lovely, and everything he was doing felt good, but my mind kept drifting away to the love that

I'd had.

"Maybe this will help you focus," Boude said as he settled himself between my legs and smiled up at me. "I promise to be mindful of my fangs."

His mouth and tongue worked on the most intimate parts of me, and it was incredible. The orgasm washed over me like a cool tide, strong but calming. It settled my mind, and my body was happy.

Boude kissed a line up my body and stopped to tease my nipples for a while. The afterglow from the orgasm faded, and I still needed more.

I gently tugged on his hair to get his attention and said, "Inside me, please."

He nipped at my skin hard enough for me to cry out, and positioned himself against me. My logical brain clicked on, and I asked, "Condom?"

"Vampires are incapable of carrying disease, and we're both dead, so pregnancy is also not a concern."

I laughed. "Makes sense."

He smiled and kissed me, his soft curls falling around us like a crimson curtain. He kissed me softly, and gently opened my mouth to his with his tongue. As he kissed me, he slid inside of me so very slowly, letting me feel each inch of him. I moaned and gasped against his mouth, but he wouldn't let me break the kiss; his tongue took over my mouth as his body took over mine. I was filled with him, and when he couldn't push into me any further, his body stilled while his mouth worked hungrily at mine.

My body spasmed around his, desperate for the motion that would get me where I wanted to be. My hips moved against his, trying to reach that one sweet spot. Finally, I could pull away enough to say, "Please,

please, fuck me."

His eyes went wide, but it was the rest of his face that showed the surprised emotion. He laughed, and it was a full, lovely sound.

"I didn't expect to hear that word come out of you," he chuckled.

I looked at him, my mouth parted and eyes wide, pleading.

He leaned over and placed his mouth to my ear. "Is this how you want me to move?" he asked, as his hips found a smooth, steady rhythm.

The feel of his breath in my ear sent shivers over my skin, and the feel of finally getting what I needed carried me far away from all the pain I had felt for so long.

CHAPTER EIGHT

Boude left after several hours of being with me. The sky still looked the same as when we had gotten here, dull and dead.

I needed to dig, to work off some of this damn time, but I hadn't wanted him to leave. I didn't seem to have "feelings" for Boude, but I felt less crazy when he was around. I had to focus on being a big girl when he left, and not begging to him to stay right with me so I didn't fall apart.

Out in the field, I dug mindlessly. I still didn't mind the work, but when I was alive it was easier to focus, to feel like I was giving someone peace. Now, digging them up from the other side, I didn't know if it was peace or heartache I was delivering.

"I can't believe you let a vampire stay with you." Soren was standing over me, his shadow eclipsing mine.

"He was kinder to me than you've been," I said.

"Vampires aren't kind," he snorted. "They want your blood, sex, or soul."

I wasn't feeling friendly, and I didn't like Soren being mean about one of the few people who had been nice to me.

"Well, I'll tell you, I had sex with him, and I think I got a lot more out of it than he did."

He scoffed, "I'm telling you, though, you better be careful," Soren warned, and walked away.

I rolled my eyes and watched him go. I looked down to see the frail little old man I had just dug up disappear in a flash. I blinked at the hole I had just dug, and filled it back in again.

Truthfully, my mind was having difficulty deciding if sex with Boude had been a good idea or not. On one hand, it had provided much needed distraction and relaxation. It was the best I had felt since I died. On the other hand, it still felt kind of wrong to be sleeping with someone who wasn't Raphael, like I should wait for him. A small part of me even felt like I didn't deserve happiness, like death should just be sorrow and suffering.

I reasoned with myself on both sides of the fence as I dug, even talking out loud and nodding at times. I was glad there weren't any other reapers around to see my breakdown, and if Soren saw, I didn't care.

When the shovel moved the last bit of dirt revealing the body beneath it, my heart sank. It was a young girl of about seventeen or eighteen. Her hair was shiny black, and cut in a cute bob with straight bangs; her dress was pale blue with a white collar that reminded me of a school uniform. Her shoes were delicate, white Mary Jane's, and looked like they pinched. Her face was perfect though: someone had really taken their time on her eyes and pink lips. She looked like an oversized children's doll.

I wondered what had happened to her. I know, of

course, kids die every day; healthy people die every day. The world has a million ways to kill us, but seeing one that died in the middle of growing up… just hurt.

I picked up my flashlight and clicked it on, hoping as I did every time, that she would just disappear—hoping her soul was settled.

She blinked at the blinding light and started crying, repeating "I did it," over and over.

I knelt down beside her. "What, honey, what did you do?"

"I died," she sighed, and I realized she wasn't upset, she was relieved.

I took her hand and smiled gently; I couldn't imagine a life so bad that you would be relieved to kill yourself.

"I have to take you into the city to get assigned, OK? You died young, so you'll have to stay between worlds a while and work off your time that you would have spent alive," I explained.

"Work? Are you freaking kidding me?" She rolled her eyes and stood up.

"I know," I shrugged. I was still in disbelief at her happiness over being dead.

She looked down at herself and wrinkled her nose. "Can I at least get some different clothes? I don't want to be in this crap *he* put me in." She made a face when she said "he."

"Sure, we can stop at a little place in town. Who put you in those clothes?" I asked.

"My 'uncle'—a family friend who took me in when my parents went to jail for drugs. He was a very wealthy dealer, who had looked at me a little too hard since I was about six. My parents were so grateful he brought me in to live in his mansion and offered to pay a tutor so that I didn't have to go through the bullying about everything at school. But he really just kept me as his personal living doll, and threatened to expose more on my parents if I didn't do the things he wanted." She made an obscene gesture with her hand towards her mouth.

I grimaced. "So you killed yourself?"

"I couldn't get outside of that damn house with all his guards and cameras, and I could only make supervised phone calls, but there were always drugs around." She smiled as if it had been the perfect plan.

My problems suddenly seemed far away. I put out my hand. "I'm Helena, Hel, for short."

She took my hand with her own, showing perfectly manicured pink nails. "I'm Grace."

Grace looked around in amazement as I walked her into the city. The gray buildings that haunted me and made me miss my home were a whole new world of freedom to her.

We stopped in the boutique to get some clothes for Grace. The blonde vampire with the amber eyes was still the one running the shop. His outfit had changed, so I assumed it was the equivalent of a different day.

"Ah, nice to see you back, Helena. And you've brought a friend." He smiled, and flashed just a hint of fang. He must practice a lot.

"This is Grace," I introduced. "And I'm sorry, I didn't get your name last time."

"Andreas," he nodded gracefully.

Grace's mouth was open. I had forgotten to tell her about vampires.

I elbowed her, and she recovered quickly, though

was obviously still enamored.

"What are you looking for, dear?" He eyed her with one hand on his hip. "Something in the way of what you have on, or…?"

Grace held up her hand to stop him. "Nothing like what I have on."

Andreas grinned, and they proceeded to bound around the store grabbing this and that, laughing and giggling like two teenagers would do.

I stood watching, letting Grace have her fun. Who knew how long, if ever, it had been since she had gotten to choose her own clothes, or make a friend.

Eventually, she settled on a plain black crop top, and a pair of high waisted red bell bottoms, with a pair of black boots that laced up the front. The outfit showed off her slim figure, and made her already long legs seem longer. She looked like a model. It was too attention-getting for me, but I hadn't been imprisoned for years and forced to wear doll clothes.

Andreas whistled and clapped when Grace walked through the store.

"Thank you so much for helping me." Grace said to the vampire, who was eyeing himself in a compact mirror. So much for that myth.

"Of course, you are fantastic. Where are you off to now?" He flipped the shiny gold compact shut and looked up at us with a brilliant smile, fangs gleaming.

"She has to get assigned," I said.

"OH!" Andreas exclaimed. "I could use help here, if you want to ask."

"Seriously?" Grace was practically ready to jump up and down.

"Seriously. I could even be your sponsor, if you

like," he added.

Grace and I said, "What?" at the same time.

Andreas smiled and nodded. "Anyone who dies under eighteen years old must have a sponsor who will watch out for them: make sure they continue to mature, help them decide about the future, etc. If they are very young, they have to live with you, but Grace can decide for herself."

"I don't mind sponsoring you, Grace. And you're welcome to live with me," I told her.

She hugged me, and then looked at Andreas, "Is it still OK if I work here?"

"Of course, we're going to be fast friends." He winked at her like another girlfriend would.

We said our goodbyes to the vampire and walked on towards the town center. The line wasn't too long right now, which was great, since I needed to get back to work. I assumed if I was going to sponsor Grace, that I needed to be with her.

Grace didn't flinch when she was told how much time she had left to work off. She had slightly fewer hours than I had, which surprised me. Apparently, Grace had shortened an already short life contract.

It was agreed she would work at Andreas's boutique, and live with me.

When we left, we stopped by another couple of stores to let Grace pick up some makeup and hair stuff that she swore was absolutely essential. We also made arrangements to have another small bed delivered to my place for her.

I was still feeling strange about the whole sleeping/ not sleeping thing here. I still wanted sleep, but never got sleepy. So, I figured having a bed for Grace was best, just in case.

As we walked back towards the fields, I could tell Grace was feeling uncomfortable.

"You really don't mind working off your time by digging up dead people?" she asked.

"I spent my time alive burying them," I laughed.

"Really?" Grace seemed shocked.

"Really, it doesn't make me uncomfortable. There's a need for it, on both sides, apparently, and it helps people."

Grace paused in thought. "Well, I'm glad you're the one who woke me up."

"Me too," I smiled.

Soren was out in front of the houses when we walked up. He shook his head when he saw Grace with me. His large arms rested on his slender waist, causing him to look like an extra large, blonde, bearded, and unhappy version of Superman.

Grace looked at the big man, and then turned over her shoulder to whisper to me, "Holy cow, he's huge! And really hot!"

A grin I couldn't control crept across my face, so I ducked my head and let us into the house. I had noticed that Soren was attractive, but I'd been a bit too repelled by his shitty attitude to think much about him.

"Wander around and make yourself at home," I told Grace. "I had better step outside and talk to Soren."

Grace agreed, opening cabinets and walking around. I went outside, where Soren was waiting for me.

Now that I had really noticed how attractive he was, maybe I wouldn't feel so intimidated by him—or, maybe it would be worse.

"You brought home another stray, I see." He shook his head. "You have work to do you know."

"I sponsored her," I said coolly.

"Hell, Helena. They have places and programs for kids like that. You'll never get your time worked off watching her." He rubbed the back of his neck like it ached.

"It's my time to waste if I want. Besides, she's already assigned to Andreas's boutique in town, so I can work while she does."

"You're crazy letting her work with a vamp. I know you don't see it yet, but they are dangerous," he said.

"You're right, I don't see it yet, and I believe in giving people, or vampires, the benefit of the doubt. When I dug her up, that girl was relieved that she had succeeded with suicide, because she was basically imprisoned as a dirty old man's sex doll. She deserves more now."

Soren sighed, rubbed the back of his neck again and turned to walk away.

CHAPTER NINE

Hours passed, days, weeks, maybe even a month; with no calendar or true nighttime, I couldn't keep track anymore. The watch on my wrist only counted the hours I worked, so it wasn't helpful.

Grace was my saving grace. My heart ached less for Raphael, I think in part because she liked hearing stories about him. My memories of him hurt beyond measure when I recalled them, but telling them out loud to Grace somehow seemed to help. She even made up stories with me about what he was doing now and how his life was going. She sometimes talked about the things she had endured in life; that was a lot harder to hear, but I figured if she had lived it, I could listen to it.

I dug while she worked, and sometimes took breaks to see Boude. He was a sweet escape from the routine I had created. The sex with him was fun: it eased the ache and left me restful, but it never lived up to my memory of Raphael. I often wondered if he had been that good, or if that was just how I wanted to remember him. I knew Raphael and I hadn't known each other long enough for him to be so important to me. But I didn't really have anyone else in the living world after Ray died, and it still felt like unfinished business.

Soren and I had become somewhat nice to each other, even making the occasional joke. I think a lot of it was for Billy. He was so kind-hearted, and it was obvious all he wanted was for everyone to get along.

One day, it was just the two of us out in the field. "How did you die?" I asked him.

His face grew serious and still. "Hunting accident."

I nodded. I didn't need to know more.

"Someone killed you, didn't they?" he asked.

"Basically." I shrugged, recalling the events that had led to my death.

It was Soren's turn to nod. There was no use for "I'm sorrys" or sharing details. It was what it was, we both left people behind that we would miss for ages, and we both ended up in the same place.

We resumed our digging, and after a time I heard Soren swear, "Ah, hell."

I knew by now that he had dug up someone that hadn't disappeared, someone that would need to be walked into the city to be assigned. Soren hated leaving the fields.

I heard a woman crying, and when I looked over, a tall blonde was clinging to Soren and sobbing onto his shoulder. It was sad of course, but after so many bodies, you become a bit numb; after all, we had all been in the same situation. I resisted the urge to laugh, but couldn't help the smirk that crossed my face.

He gently put a hand on the woman's back and made an awkward "there there" gesture. I was impressed as I heard Soren trying to soothe the poor woman. The moment was all too brief, though, as he walked her over to me and said, "This nice woman is Helena, she will take you into town and get you settled."

I glared at him as I took the woman's hand. Soren had to unlatch her from himself as I tried to lead her away. Once she was beside me, I tossed my shovel at him, none too gently.

"I'm going to stop by the boutique and check on Grace on my way back," I said to Soren.

He smiled and waved me off.

One thing I hadn't been able to figure out was the fact that, even in death, I couldn't understand other languages. Shouldn't that be some kind of perk that comes with living in the after world? The poor lady walked beside me going on and on in another tongue, looking at me for a glint of understanding, and all I could do was nod and pat her hand. It was damn frustrating.

I got her to the assignment line in record time, and luckily it was short. She seemed to understand she needed to stay there, and as I walked away, I heard another person speaking her language. I let out a sigh and wandered a few streets over to the shops and cafes.

The sky was the same dull gray as always, and the air held no chill or warmth. I was used to it now, but I still would have given anything to feel the wind.

I picked up two vanilla coffees at the coffee shop, and then wandered into the boutique.

A woman about my age was at the counter, with platinum blonde hair and big breasts. I hadn't seen her in here before. She looked friendly but a little distracted, doodling on a sheet of paper.

"Hi, is Grace around?" I smiled at the blonde.

"She's in the back," the blonde offered, and stayed perched on her stool.

I nodded and smiled, staring back at her to see if she'd get the hint.

"Oh, would you like me to get her for you?" she asked.

"That would be great."

She trotted off to the back, and in a moment, Grace came out front. Grace smiled when she saw me, and happily took the coffee I was holding out to her.

"Who's the new girl?" I asked.

"Barbie," Grace laughed, "Not even kidding."

I laughed, too. "Where is Andreas?"

I had been into the store more than a few times at this point, and had never not seen him here.

"He's with Boude, above ground," she said as she straightened up the front counter.

I'm sure I looked puzzled for a moment before it hit me. "Oh, vampire things."

Boude never really talked about things like that when we were together. I didn't know how it all worked. I knew he needed living blood to survive, and I knew that meant going to the "above ground" world, but I hadn't truly understood it. Boude had previously mentioned he and Andreas were friends. I thought it was cool that my two vampires friends were also friends with each other.

"How often does Andreas go?" I asked.

"Whenever he gets hungry or bored, I guess. Sometimes it's daily, sometimes it's every few days," said Grace. "He makes it look pretty good, and there's a part of me that would love to go back and tear out that bastard's throat."

I certainly understood the appeal of wanting to go back. "Does Andreas kill people?" I asked.

"I've asked him; he said he has, but doesn't always. He can feed without killing, and without the person remembering, so that's what he usually does. Seems like a pretty sweet deal to me." Grace smiled.

I could see the wheels turning in her mind. She wanted to be changed. "You wouldn't want to sacrifice your soul, would you?" As appealing as vampirism was, I just felt like my soul was too important to cast aside.

"What's it done for me lately? It's never protected me, fed me, or kept me warm when I was forced to sleep on the cold tile for disobeying," she shrugged.

I had a bad feeling she was talking herself into this instead of out of it.

"Yeah, but if you're a vampire, you have to live where the rest of them live," I shuddered. "That place is creepy."

"I've been over with Andreas to his place. No one bothered me, since I was a friend of his, and inside, his place is really beautiful."

"Are you sleeping with Andreas?" The words were out of my mouth before I had a chance to stop them or think them through.

Grace chuckled. "No, none of us sleep," she said.

"Grace…" I said, hoping she'd volunteer more.

"Does Andreas strike you as the type of vampire who would like sex with women?" Grace patted my hand.

I laughed at my silliness, hugged her, and headed back to the field, a little relieved, but still uneasy.

Soren was still digging when I got back. I retrieved my shovel from where he had dropped it after I tossed it to him. I began digging, but felt more than a little distracted.

I caught Soren watching me out of the corner of his eye. I turned to look at him in a, "Yes, can I help you?" kind of way.

He furrowed his brow and stiffened. "You OK?" he asked. "You seem like something's bothering you since you got back."

I hesitated to tell Soren, knowing his already strong distaste for vampires. But, if we were going to be friends he would just have to accept that I was friends with some of them.

I stood up straight and looked at him, thought about what I wanted to say, and bit my lip. I put my shovel against the dead dirt and shoved it in with my foot, looking down.

"I'm afraid Grace will let them turn her," I said, with a rather large lump in my throat.

I could have sworn I felt heat coming off of Soren like a furnace—anger, so much anger.

He was gripping the handle of his shovel so hard I expected it to snap. I had to give him credit, though, his face was damn near expressionless.

"I don't need an 'I told you so.'" I rolled my eyes and tried to keep any surprise tears pushed back.

His face softened, looking at me. "Hel, if I had come over at her age, in her circumstances, I probably would have crossed without a second thought."

I knew it must have taken a lot for him to have said that in such a cool manner. I walked over to him and wrapped my arms around him in a hug. His body stilled, but I didn't let go. "Thank you," I said, and he softened and hugged me back.

We resumed our work, and after a while Billy joined us. Billy always tried to make the best out of working, so he was always singing, whistling, or humming some kind of silly folk song or made up tune.

Most days Soren and I just listened to him, but he started singing a catchy little tune we had heard him sing many times before, and soon we were all singing along while we dug. We were happy little reapers.

CHAPTER TEN

I NOW KNEW HOW MEN FELT WHEN THEY had gotten tangled up in my hair while we were in bed. Boude's hair was wrapped around my fingers, and somehow still in my face. I got myself loose and laughed.

"My apologies, even in death it has a mind of its own," he said, and tried to pull the red curls back behind him.

His comment raised a question. "Do you still consider yourself dead, even though you're a vampire?"

"My heart doesn't beat, I can't walk in the sunlight, and I've suffered a mortal's death. Hard to say I'm not dead, don't you think?" He ran his fingers softly up and down my arm.

I nodded, but was quiet.

"What's weighing on you sweet, Hel?"

When I didn't answer after a moment, he turned my face to his and kissed my forehead.

When I opened my eyes, I was staring into two endless pools of emerald. I didn't think I'd ever get used to vampire eyes, but it wasn't as awkward as it was at first.

"Grace is thinking of letting Andreas bring her over," I said.

"And you are unhappy about this?" he asked.

"Of course. I don't want her to give up her soul."

The vampire rolled onto his back and seemed to contemplate this for a long while. "Soul's are really an over-valued thing. They're fine if you want to serve a god or be a ghost, or just know for certain a part of you will always exist. Other than that, they don't really do anything," he mused. "Why are you so attached to her keeping hers if she doesn't want it?"

It was my turn to stop and think. I wanted to give an answer that didn't involve religion, since I knew that wouldn't matter to him in the least. "Isn't your soul, in a sense, your conscience, the thing that gives you your humanity?"

"Perhaps it is the brain that does that, but say you're right. Look at me: am I a monster with no sense of duty?" he asked.

"Well, you don't seem to be," I said.

He laughed his was a warm, deep laugh. It made me smile, and I kissed him. He kissed me back, and was soon on top of me, ready to end our serious conversation.

"Can you do something for me?" I asked.

He nuzzled my ear, whispered, "Yes, I can do that thing that you like," and his hand slid down my body.

"Not that," I laughed. "Well, not yet. First, can you promise me you'll try to dissuade Grace from changing?"

"If I see her, I will be certain to tell her of the potential downside to being a vampire. That's the best I can do. I will ultimately leave the decision to her," he said.

I pressed my lips together in a tight line, and tried to decide if that was a good enough promise. But then his fingers did the thing that I liked, and I couldn't think any longer.

In life, I had never been one for casual sex. Shouldn't something so extremely intimate be guarded and shared only with those who are truly special? Here, I didn't have the heart to care.

Sex made me feel good; it was one of the few things that did, and Boude made me feel special. There was no hope in the slightest of us falling in love with one another. Whatever that spark was that two people needed for the "L" word to come up, we didn't have it. That was ok with me, though. Love was the last thing I wanted; it hurt too much.

I was at the door, saying goodbye to Boude, when Grace came walking up. She smiled coyly at the two of us and slipped by.

"Thanks for coming to see me," I whispered to him.

"It was a pleasure, as always," Boude said, and the curve of his smile gave away that he thought of making some kind of inappropriate remark, but censored himself.

He kissed my fingers lightly and left.

I stepped in and closed the door.

"So, you've had a good day," Grace called from her bed.

"Mmhm, I have." I sighed and crawled back into the covers.

"Is sex really that fun?" Grace asked.

I turned to look at her, puzzled.

She began talking again before I could answer. "I mean, I've had sex, but I was too young to understand it. I just remember it being gross and painful."

My heart ached for her. No matter how much of her story I knew, you just never became used to hearing a young girl talk about being abused.

"With the right person, it's none of those things," I said, hoping that was a good answer. "Do you have someone you're thinking of being with?" I asked.

She chuckled. "Hell no. But maybe one day I'd like to try it again."

"Well, whenever you do, I hope you have a marvelous time," I said.

"Yeah, me too," she added, and I heard the longing in her voice.

We both laid there a long while, then I decided I should work.

I was alone out in the fields. That hadn't happened in a while—someone was always around, usually Billy or Soren, but sometimes other reapers as well. This seemed to be the profession for introverts. None of us talked very much, and we minded our own business— well, except for Soren's interest in my personal affairs. But he was getting better.

The fields of dead stretched before me in an ocean of brown dirt, until brown and gray met at the horizon, in a murky, muddy color that made me sigh. I dug, and tried not to think too hard about anything serious. I started singing one of the songs I had heard from

Billy, and smiled to myself.

A silhouette of someone in the distance caught my eye. The hair was wild, and the figure was hunched forward. I noticed the oddly shaped, gangly limbs even though the person didn't seem very tall. The movements were slow some moments, and erratic at others.

Someone freaked out when they woke and ran from their reaper, I thought. It made sense, I could easily see it happening. A little old person who died confused, wakes up to a bright light in their face in a field of dirt. Yep, it happened.

"Hey there!" I called out, trying to offer help and a friendly voice. "Do you need some help?"

The person didn't answer, they just continued to make small erratic movements.

I walked toward the confused person, wondering where on earth their reaper was? I couldn't figure out how he had gotten that far away.

"Where is your reaper?" I asked.

I was about twenty feet away when I realized who was wandering around the fields of the dead. That was about twenty feet too close when he saw me.

Rasputin's white hair was in stringy patches on top of his head, and his endless black eyes locked on mine. I had thought he was terrifying in the shadows of the Quarter. He was even scarier in the light where I could see him clearly.

There was something so much worse about monsters that could get you anytime.

"Oh shit," I said out loud, as I tried to figure out my best course of action. Just because I couldn't die again didn't mean I wanted to feel him tearing my throat out.

"Blood." He smiled, showing fangs so decayed and discolored, I wondered how they didn't fall out.

I swallowed hard and couldn't blink. The emptiness in my hand registered in my mind. I had dropped my damn shovel back where I was digging. I had no weapons, and even dead, I didn't have the strength to fight a vampire—even a crazy vampire.

"My blood is dead, it's no good to you," I said, in as calm a tone as I could manage without screaming, praying someone would hear me. I was taking small steps backwards.

"Dead blood is still blood," he said with a nod, and took steps towards me.

"Boude told you to leave me alone, remember? In the alley, he told you I'm his friend." I stepped back again.

Rasputin seemed to stop and think a moment, then seemed to agree. "Yes, friend of Boude, who I followed here. I will not harm you, I will be... gentle." He said gentle like it should make everything OK. He extended a bony hand my way, and his long, sharp nails nearly closed the gap between us.

Nausea swirled its way around my stomach, and I knew there would be no talking my way out of this. I let out the longest, loudest, scream for help that I could manage and turned to run.

I didn't hear his footfalls behind me, didn't hear his breath, or sense the weight of him against my back. I only felt the hair being brushed off my neck as I ran. I glanced over one shoulder to see him flying weightlessly right along beside me, and just as I noticed him, he struck.

His fangs were in my neck before he could even pin me down, and yet I couldn't move. I could hear him slurping and feel him sucking, while a part of him I didn't even want to think about grew hard against my leg.

I was food, and sex, and I wished in that moment that I could die again.

I didn't know how much time had passed when the vampire finally released me and screeched in pain.

Small arms wrapped around me from behind and pulled me back from the screaming Rasputin. It was Grace.

She took off her over-shirt and held it to my neck, and we watched as Soren knocked the vampire to the ground, and impaled him with the broken wooden handle of a shovel.

Rasputin froze like we had just dipped him in nitroglycerine, but he didn't die. He made an unending growling noise, and threw in the occasional hiss through gritted teeth.

"You staked him, why didn't he die?" Grace asked.

Soren stared down at the immobile vampire. "You know, I'm not sure."

"Grace, run to the boutique and tell Andreas what's going on. Get him to send Boude out here as fast as he can," I said.

Grace nodded and took off.

Soren nudged Rasputin with his boot, and seemed satisfied that he couldn't attack or get away. He walked over sat down next to me. He took away the shirt that I had been holding to my neck and looked at the wound.

"It's not too bad, it's stopped bleeding," he said.

"You held still when he bit and didn't run, so the skin didn't tear too badly."

I nodded and replayed the whole scene in my head; I had known better than to pull away from the vampire. I remembered Rasputin's words: " friend of Boude, who I followed here."

Not long ago a realization like that would have made me cry, but not now. I was angry at myself, at my selfishness, at my stupidity.

I took a deep breath that shook through my insides, and glanced at Soren. His large gray eyes were fixed on me, and for the first time I appreciated the beauty in those human eyes.

Finally, I choked getting the words out. "He followed Boude here. It could've been Grace, or you, or Billy or any of the other reapers that he attacked." My voice was stern. I had done something bad; I didn't deserve the luxury of self-pity. "I'm sorry. I won't invite Boude over again if you let me stay on here," I added. Soren had every right to tell me to get reassigned.

"You did an idiotic thing by bringing a vampire into the fields," he said.

I dropped my head, but then he went on.

"And from your stupid mistake, I learned Boude isn't such a bad guy, er, vamp. Maybe not all vampires are monsters. You also learned that some are. I guess we were both right. And I don't know of a single person, living or dead, that hasn't fucked up something at some point." He chuckled.

In that moment, looking at Soren, I saw past his size, his rough exterior. I saw that he had a big gooey center. A Viking of a man, who no doubt would have sat down with his little girls and played tea party every night.

"So you'll let me stay?" I asked, feeling more hope than I should have.

"Of course," he said.

I moved closer to him, and he put his arm around me. It wasn't a romantic gesture, just a friendly one, and I needed his friendship right now.

Boude, Andreas, and Grace came walking through the fields. They glanced over at the nearly petrified body of Rasputin, who was still making a gurgling sound. One held an expression of anger on his face, and the other wore a look of sadness.

Boude came to me with an extended hand, pulled me up onto my feet, and hugged me. He gingerly examined the wound on my neck with his fingers, and hugged me again.

"I am so sorry this happened to you," he said.

"I'm OK. Thanks for coming," I whispered.

"What do we do with this one?" Soren's low voice grumbled.

Boude and I turned to see everyone else standing over Rasputin.

Boude and Andreas moved together so they could discuss vampire things.

"He was supposed to stay in the confines of the Vampire Quarter; he was supposed to honor my words not to harm you." Boude nodded my direction; his face held more emotion than I could ever recall seeing.

Andreas added, "His brain and body are sick with disease because he hasn't been able to get living blood in so long."

"Why can't he get living blood?" I asked.

Boude filled us in. "In the above world, he was captured, nearly a century ago. Instead of killing him, they wrapped him in silver chains, starved him, and locked him inside a coffin hidden away in a cave. So when he goes to the above world, he is trapped, with no access to fresh blood. His body still burns with silver, yet he doesn't die. He consumes blood in this world just to take the edge off of his hunger, but as you've seen, dead blood has some ill effects."

"Wait, so you have two bodies? One here and one up there?" I couldn't quite wrap my head around the concept.

"Think of it as a very real extension or projection. The two are separate, but part of a whole," Andreas tried to explain.

I nodded in understanding, but I'm certain my face still looked puzzled.

"We can leave him as he is, and put his body somewhere where it will not be bothered. Or, we can go to the location of Rasputin's body in the above world, and end his turmoil for good," said Boude, with a small ounce of pity in his voice.

"You mean kill him? What was he like before the dead blood?" I asked Boude.

"I didn't know him long before he became what he is. He took me in after the vampire who turned me died. We hunted together, and had many long talks. Soon after, it was me caring for him." Boude's face was solemn.

Soren's deep voice broke the heavy silence. "If he were to be freed in the above world and receive living blood, would he become himself again?"

"It's a thought. Many vampires have recovered from

their captures, but I know none that were as far gone as him," said Boude.

"Has no one ever tried to rescue him before?" I asked.

Boude and Andreas looked at each other, then at me. "It would be challenging to find where he is locked away," said Boude.

"Dangerous?" I bit my lip as I looked at the impaled vampire on the ground. He had stopped screeching, and was simply staring up at the sky, a look of surrender on his face. I didn't want to feel sorry for him, but knowing his story now, it was hard not to care.

I looked back to the functional vampires standing beside me. They gave a single nod in unison as an answer to my question.

I didn't know how to feel about them going on this kind of mission. They were my friends. I hated the thought of them risking their lives, but something had to be done. And I didn't think any of us had hearts hard enough to leave Rasputin a prisoner of his own body in both worlds.

We were all quiet for a moment, then Boude and Andreas nodded at each other. They took Rasputin under each of his arms and carried him off toward the Quarter.

They stopped in front of me, and Boude said, "I'm so sorry this happened, Helena. We will discuss the best course of action, and I'll let you know what we decide."

I watched them walk away, and turned back to look at Grace and Soren. Grace came to me and hugged me, and Soren eyed me with a look that said he was waiting for me to cry.

I took a deep breath that was steadier than I expected it to be, and walked back over to the spot where I had stopped digging a short time ago.

Grace said something to Soren that I couldn't quite hear, and out of the corner of my eye I saw him nod. She went back towards our house, and in a moment, Soren was quietly digging beside me.

I let him continue a while, catching him checking on me every little bit.

"I'm fine," I said as I tossed a shovel full of dirt to the side. "I will not break," I reassured myself as well as him.

"I see that. Hel, you're a lot tougher than I would have ever imagined," he said, and I saw kindness in his eyes, along with something new, but I couldn't tell if it was respect or pity. I hoped it was respect.

I didn't know if he was using my name or the expletive, but it didn't really matter. I just let out a small, "Thanks," and kept digging.

As usual, I tried to push back all the scary thoughts, all the sad thoughts, while I worked. I didn't want to think about being attacked by Rasputin, although part of me wanted to know what would have happened if he had really gotten to me. Even though I couldn't die again, it had been a terrifying experience. I thought about asking Soren, but I just didn't have the energy to speak.

The next thoughts seemed to sneak up on me. I was replaying my few short weeks with Raphael, all from the beginning. The lump in my throat and hot tears in my eyes brought me back to reality. I tried with all my might to stop thinking about that life before we got to my death. I couldn't seem to redirect my thoughts, though, and it all just kept playing like a movie in my head: the kisses, the sex, the planning of our trip, and losing it all.

"God dammit," I said, and threw down my shovel. I could see that I had almost uncovered a body, but I just couldn't finish right now. No one needed a hysterical reaper waking them up in the afterlife.

I sat down in the dirt with my head in my hands. I didn't care who could see me or what they thought. I had pushed it all so far back that I couldn't hold anymore, and it was coming out now.

I heard the sound of the shovel in the dirt, and looked up to see Billy finishing what I had started.

"Thanks, Billy," I said, and tried to give him a half smile.

"Aw, it's nothing. You've had a hard day." He smiled at me and rubbed his neck.

Looking up at him was like looking at a telephone pole, scrawny and tall.

"I think I have hard days a little too frequently," I moaned.

"It ain't exactly the easy life here," he chuckled. "Go see Soren, get him to pour you a drink."

I started to say no, but then thought, *Why not?*

"Thanks, Billy. I appreciate you." I gave him a kiss on the cheek as I walked by, and he even blushed a little.

I walked over to the row of houses. I walked by Soren's place all the time, but couldn't recall ever knocking on his door. His was number three.

I paused for a moment, then knocked lightly and leaned against the wall beside the door.

I heard heavy footsteps coming my way, and the door opened. He didn't seem surprised to see me, but smirked at me laying against his doorway.

I rolled my head up to look at him. "Billy said you'd make me a drink."

"Come in," he said, and walked back inside.

His place was plain but clean—probably cleaner than my place was at the moment.

"Gin or whiskey?" he asked.

"Gin, please," I answered, and took a seat at his table without him offering.

He set a gin and tonic down in front of me, complete with lime. I sipped it; the drink was refreshing, and heavy on the gin.

"Thanks," I said, taking a long drink of the beverage.

"Of course." He sipped his whiskey neat.

"How do you keep it together here?" I asked, once the warmth of the alcohol ran through me. I didn't understand how I could be dead and drunk, but I was so damn tired of trying to figure out the rules of this place.

"I was angry for a long time, still kind of am. But there ain't a damn thing I can do to fix it, so I'm trying not be as upset." Soren shrugged his big shoulders.

His eyes were soft, and a little sad; I stared into them, and he into mine.

He broke the gaze with a wink and took a sip of his drink. "Besides, you're tougher than me, anyway."

I laughed, and it caught me off guard. "How do you figure that?"

"I push everyone away so I don't have to feel anything extra. Your heart was shattered, but you keep reaching out. No matter what has happened to you here, you get out and dig. That takes balls," he smiled.

I pulled the neck of my shirt out and looked down at my boobs. I tried to think of something smart to say, but the alcohol had dulled my wit and nothing came to mind, so I just looked up at Soren blankly.

He laughed until his cheeks were pink and he had to wipe a tear from his eye. I laughed at myself a little too, though I didn't find it nearly as funny as he did.

"It's really nice to see you laugh," I said with the first genuine smile I had felt on my face in ages.

"It's been a while since I've laughed that hard," he said as he straightened himself out to regain his composure. He got up and walked to the sink, he rinsed out his glass, but then poured himself another drink.

I walked up behind him to ask for a refill, not meaning to be quiet or sneaky, but when he turned around he was surprised to see me standing so close.

He stepped a few inches closer, and we stayed there. We looked into each other's eyes and felt the tension between us like the surface of water. We were floating so close, and all it would take was one tiny movement for us both to sink under the surface.

Of course I thought he was attractive: he was big and safe and strong, but he was also an asshole most of the time. I knew I could rely on him, but this was a bad idea, wasn't it?

He was so different from Raphael, from Boude. Gee, I had been getting around lately. I'd have to have a stern talk with myself about that when I was sober.

Soren licked his lips in a small, unsure flick of his tongue, and I started to raise up to close the distance, no longer caring if it was a good idea or a bad one.

In that moment, Soren stepped back, and I was left alone, nearly on tip toes, waiting for a kiss I wasn't going to get.

I watched him pour out his whiskey and get a drink of water.

"I should probably go help Billy. I feel a little bad with him being out there by himself," Soren said. His voice was grumbly, but I could hear the uncertainty he was trying to hide.

"Sure," I said, and placed my glass in the sink. "Thanks for the drink." I walked towards the door, my buzz suddenly nowhere to be found.

"Anytime," Soren replied, and walked out with me.

He took off towards the field, and I wandered back to my own place, still confused, but not as shaken. I tried not to give it too much thought. It was just a nearly drunken kiss between two coworkers, no more, no less. *Probably a good thing he stopped it*, I told myself.

CHAPTER ELEVEN

I KEPT MYSELF AT MY OWN PLACE FOR A WHILE, so as not to risk ending up in some new bizarre situation.

I waited eagerly for Grace to get home. I wanted to see if she knew anything about Boude and Andreas's decision. I questioned how much I should really get involved with the people here. It was one thing to make friends, but maybe Soren's approach was better. I needed to work my time off, and move on. Did I really need to trouble myself about things that didn't concern me? Maybe that was just my humanity speaking. But wasn't I still technically human?

Ray came to mind, his voice echoing in my head. It had been too long since I had heard it. "Helena, it's never only about you. If you have a choice help, always help."

I sighed and wondered where he was. For all I knew, maybe he was working at a shop down the street, or maybe he had made peace with God and moved on. I wished I could see him and hug him, but all of that seemed so far behind me.

I buzzed around my place, cleaning things that were

already clean, and imagining decorating the space with things I'd never go into town and actually get. I always had better things to do, but I guess I was just trying to distract myself from the day I'd had.

When the knock at my door came, I opened it without stopping to wonder who it could be. It was Boude.

I smiled at the red headed vampire, and didn't stop myself from stepping in to kiss him. I hadn't realized how much I was craving closeness with someone— although I suppose I should have, after my near miss with Soren.

Boude kissed me back, and for a change, he was being the gentle one. When my fingers twisted in his red curls and I pressed my body against him as close as I could get, his hands on my shoulders gently pushed me back.

He broke the kiss, and I looked at him inquisitively. The look on his face was one I hadn't seen before. I'd seen him be smug, and seductive (which was my favorite); I had seen anger, and tenderness. The look on his face now wiped the smile from mine: he looked afraid.

My libido sank like a stone. "What's wrong, Boude?"

"It's Grace: Andreas is turning her." His voice was almost timid.

"Take me to her," I demanded.

"I don't know if that's a good idea. I just thought you should know," he said. Boude was still standing in the doorway, and I could tell he was trying to decide whether he should step inside, or back out. He settled for staying put.

"Take me to her, or I'll just look for her myself," I

said as I pushed past him going out the door.

He nodded in defeat and we headed off to the Quarter.

Neither of us said anything for a few blocks, but it was Boude who finally broke the silence.

"What are you planning to do?" he asked. "I don't think you can talk her out of turning, and it might already be too late."

"I don't know yet but I need to be there with her." I kept my gaze forward and was walking so fast I was nearly jogging. Boude kept up easily, and looked much more graceful than me.

The entrance to the Quarter from this side was large and striking. The towering structures had sharp and intricate architecture, dark and nearly as glossy as obsidian standing out against the pale gray, boxy buildings that surrounded it. It looked like we were walking into some kind of cathedral for the damned— it kind of felt like that too. But it was not a holy place we were entering, just another area of the city. There were alleys and apartments and a few questionable vampiric businesses that I would probably never enter.

"Are we going to your place or Andreas's?" I asked.

"Andreas's; it's just ahead."

The alley narrowed, and suddenly we were climbing stairs. Everything in the Quarter looked so similar I didn't know how they found their way around. It was all darkness and sharp angles.

I had noticed there weren't any other vampires out on the streets with us, but I felt there were eyes on us—on me—everywhere.

Boude halted and knocked at a black door that I

hadn't even seen. Upon closer inspection, I saw the door had a black door knocker with a lion's head. It was only a moment before the door opened and Andreas was standing there.

He didn't look thrilled to see me, but invited us in with a well practiced wave of his hand.

"You just had to fetch her, didn't you?" Andreas asked bleakly.

"She cares for Grace; she deserves to be here," replied Boude.

I let the "fetching" comment slide, even though it annoyed me. I stepped inside, and would have laughed if I wasn't so concerned for my friend. It looked exactly like what I would have imagined a vampire's apartment to look like.

The drapes over the windows were heavy crimson velvet, tied with gold rope. Red and gold seemed to be the theme of the room, from the wallpaper, down to the uncomfortable but elegant velvet couch, and plush, old-world rug. It should have been too much for the senses, but it felt luxurious: like stepping into the home of royalty.

After looking around, I turned to the vampires and asked, "So where is she? Am I too late?"

Grace emerged from a dark wooden doorway my eyes had overlooked. Something so plain disappeared in a room with so much... well, just so much.

I went to her and hugged her, holding her too tight, and continued to hold her even when she pushed against me.

When I finally released her there were tears in her eyes. "Are you angry with me?"

"No, of course not. I just don't want you to make a

decision you'll regret," I told her.

"I'm sure this is what I want. Really and truly." She squeezed my hands and looked me in the eyes with a fierce determination.

I nodded in understanding. "But you know, there is no going back."

"I do."

"Can I stay and be with you?" I asked.

Grace turned to look at Andreas and Boude for an answer to my question.

"As long as you don't interfere, I don't see the harm," Andreas relented, but wasn't excited for my presence.

I sighed, grateful. "How dangerous is the process?"

"It can be quite dangerous: if you take all the blood, then the soul blinks out of existence before a new type of life takes over. In that case they are just... gone. But if you leave just a drop of their blood, and then give them vampire blood, the soul fades slowly as the new life takes over," Boude explained.

I could feel the worry written all over my face.

"I've successfully brought over dozens," Andreas reassured me.

Grace smiled and raised her eyebrows in an excited look that would have seemed more appropriate before getting on a roller-coaster, rather than having her blood drained from her body. But I forced my own smile and tried my best to hide the worry in my eyes. I had never had the chance to be a mother, so I knew I didn't really understand what it was to worry. I loved Grace though, and I wanted her to do whatever would make her eternity happy, especially since her living days had been such hell.

Boude and Andreas spread a soft fur blanket on the floor, and then placed a red silk pillow on top of the blanket.

Andreas offered a hand to Grace. "Are you ready?" he asked.

Grace took a deep breath and nodded, taking his hand.

Boude closed the drapes while Andreas helped Grace get comfortable on the floor. The room was suddenly darker, and small flickering lamps I hadn't noticed before now cast soft shadows on the walls, reflecting the shining gold accents scattered around the room.

I hadn't even realized I was still standing until Boude took my arm and led me to the couch.

"You'll want to sit," he said. "This takes a while."

I sat without taking my eyes off the floor, but when Boude tried to take his hand back, I squeezed it. He understood without a word, and held my hand with a gentle but reassuring grip.

Andreas gazed down at Grace, and if I hadn't known that Andreas was gay it would have looked very much like they were about to make love. This seemed nearly as intimate, just without us getting glimpses of their naughty bits.

"I won't lie, Grace. This will be painful at first, but the pain will fade quickly, and you will feel," he paused searching for the word, "euphoric."

"I'm not afraid," Grace said.

Knowing her history, I imagined the only thing Grace would fear was being alive once more, trapped back inside that fancy prison.

Andreas brushed Grace's hair behind her ear, and

gently lifted her head in his arm, exposing her neck. He smiled down at her and she squeezed her eyes shut.

"Relax," he whispered.

She sighed, and some of the tension she was holding visibly eased. He leaned his body over hers, and I could only tell he had bitten her by the small pained look on her face.

Her face softened, and she sank into Andreas's arms. He drank, and drank, and drank from her.

A thought occurred to me, and I whispered to Boude, "Won't it harm Andreas to be drinking from her?"

"He isn't drinking from her for sustenance, and he's fed from living blood not long ago, so he will be fine," Boude whispered to me so softly that I could only just hear.

Andreas was still silently drinking from my friend, and I was having trouble just watching him do so. As I touched my neck and felt the bandage I had put on my bite from Rasputin, I flinched. "Boude, where is Rasputin, and what have you all decided to do about him?" I asked.

He hadn't been moving beside me, yet somehow, he became more still. I took that as a sign he wasn't really wanting to answer my questions.

"Boude," I said, trying to spur a reaction from him.

He cleared his throat: a sound very un-vampiric. "Rasputin is still restrained in one of Andreas's back bedrooms. Once Grace has transitioned, she wants to accompany us on our journey to free his other form."

I felt my face get hot, and the room swayed. "No, no, you are not taking her with you," I said through gritted teeth. My voice was still louder than it should have been.

"It is ultimately her decision. She made the offer, Andreas and I will have to have help, and no one else will go with us. You know we will protect her," said Boude.

I knew it was true that they would watch out for her, but I shuddered at the thought of it all. I also hated the fact that I was in the same house as Rasputin, even if he couldn't get to me.

"Won't she have a super bloodlust once she is brought over?" I asked thinking of vampire books I had read through the years.

"She will be hungry, yes. But it's much easier to control it here, where living blood isn't as attainable."

"OK, but what about when you take your journey to the above world?"

"We will keep a close watch on her, and make sure she is adequately fed to stave off unmanageable cravings," he said.

I could already see I would not win this. I wasn't happy about it, but there was nothing I could do, so I sat and tried to turn off my thoughts.

Andreas finally released Grace and gently laid her on the pillow. With his back still to us I saw him bring his wrist up to his face, and then place it over Grace's mouth. In the candlelight, the vampire's blood running down her face looked like thick, sticky tar.

When he thought she'd had enough, he pulled back and covered her with another fur blanket, then turned to us with a smile. The smile was meant to give us relief, and let us know the process had gone smoothly. Since his hair was disheveled and his face was covered in a mixture of Grace's blood and his own, it was more unsettling than reassuring.

Andreas pushed himself over and leaned against the couch while staying seated on the floor. He seemed tired and sated. He licked at his wounded wrist like a bathing cat. I could tell we were waiting for Grace to wake up.

Seeing her lifeless body there on the floor was hard—even though I knew she was going to be maybe even more alive than me when she woke up, in a way.

"Are you sure she'll wake up?" The question was directed at either vampire that wanted to answer.

"Yes, I'm sure. Just give her time," Andreas replied.

After a few more moments of silence, Grace's eyelids popped open, and she looked at us. Her eyes were deep, drowning pools of honey colored amber, just like Andreas's.

Andreas smiled and nearly giggled in excitement. "Hello, little one," he cooed as if he were talking to a small child.

Grace's eyes were wide and wild, like a caged lion.

I leaned forward and spoke her name softly, "Grace, honey, are you okay?"

Her eyes shifted to me in a blink, and her head moved up and down following her gaze, but she said nothing.

Boude squeezed my hand, but moved forward on the couch, so that if the baby vampire lunged for me, he would be between us.

I was suddenly aware I could be in real danger.

"Some vampires have a little trouble transitioning. She'll be fine after she has some living blood," Andreas commented. Then he asked, "Boude, would you like to accompany us for the baby's first meal?"

"Certainly, if you could give me a few minutes to take Helena home," Boude replied.

I had to admit I was relieved. I didn't want to be alone right now, walking back through the quarter, and definitely not left alone here with Rasputin somewhere in the house.

"Ah well, hurry. She needs to eat soon." Andreas smiled as he looked at Grace, who was making a very low growling sound.

Boude looked at me and tried to hide the concern in his eyes.

"If you can just walk me to the edge of the Quarter, I can get myself back to the fields," I said.

His relief was plain. "Yes, that would be an excellent compromise, if you are comfortable with that."

"It's fine," I said, trying to make my voice match my words.

I waved to Andreas and Grace, and we headed back out into the street.

"When will you all be leaving on your expedition to find Rasputin's body?" I asked.

"As soon as Grace is herself again, and can feed properly. The first time is the hardest."

"So, you both are taking her to the living world to feed?" I asked, even though I already knew the answer.

"Yes." Boude stretched out the word like he was waiting for another question to answer.

"Are you going to let her kill someone?"

"No, we haven't killed in a long time. We usually feed on the intoxicated or the sleeping: the whole thing seems like a dream, and no one is harmed." He touched my shoulder.

We were at the end of the Quarter and stopped

walking.

I nodded. "Please look out for her. And let me see her before you leave on your quest."

Boude kissed me on the cheek. "Of course, sweet, Hel."

And with that, we both turned and went opposite ways.

CHAPTER TWELVE

I WASN'T QUITE READY TO HEAD BACK TO THE fields. I didn't want to see Soren or Billy. My mood was strange. I was happy Grace had gotten what she wanted, even if I wasn't sure I agreed with her choice. I felt down, grumpy. Why was I angry?

After wandering around the town for a while I realized I wasn't angry: I was jealous... Jealous that Grace got to go back to the world of the living as something more powerful, something that could seek revenge, if that's what she decided. No, I still wasn't willing to give up my soul for the experience, but I could envy her for doing it.

I thought about how it would feel to go back and see Raphael. I imagined him seeing me as a vampire, and all the different reactions he could have: everything from him running in fear, to him wanting me to bring him over, all the way to him staking me. Sometimes thinking about him didn't hurt quite as much, but I still missed the hell out of him.

As I walked through the city, I decided to do some window shopping. One of the home stores had a big fluffy white duvet on display that drew me in.

I couldn't stop running my hands over it, and I still hadn't picked up anything to make my apartment a cozier place. So, I had the girl at the counter bag it up for me. I couldn't get over not paying for things, but there was no rich or poor here—no classes at all, it seemed. I thanked her and headed back to the fields, feeling a little brighter at least.

"Hey, Hel," called, Billy.

"Hey, Billy," I called back.

"Whatcha got in the bag?" he asked.

"A new duvet for my bed," I smiled.

He scratched his head and narrowed his squinty eyes, until he realized what I was talking about, then nodded.

"I just wanted something to keep me warm and cozy for a change, even if I don't sleep here," I added.

"Yeah, I tried sleeping when I first got here." He shook his head and a look of unease fell on his face. "Worst nightmares I ever had."

I gave him a sympathetic smile. "Nah, I wouldn't want to risk that either."

"You coming out to dig?" he asked.

"Um, yeah, I might as well," I answered, realizing I still didn't really want to be by myself.

It was a funny thing: in life, I was such a solitary person. I loved living alone, working alone, or when it was just Ray and me. Here, I seemed to prefer company—sort of, sometimes—oh, hell, I didn't know.

Once home, I went inside and put my new duvet on the bed, after taking off the blanket that was on there from when I moved in. I smiled and looked forward to the next time I got to crawl underneath the covers. For a moment, I let myself miss Raphael and wish he could share my bed again, then I sighed and headed out to work.

Soren and Billy were digging next to each other. I chose a spot beside them, and we all seemed to fall into a steady rhythm. The awkwardness seemed to be lessening between Soren and me. Though, I had to wonder if that had been the end of the tension between us, or maybe just the beginning.

I dug and thought of Grace and her vampire guardians. I hoped her first feeding was going well, without lingering too much in thinking about the process. I wondered when they'd be coming to say they were leaving for their expedition.

A small thought flickered, wondering if I would get to give Boude a proper goodbye before such a dangerous mission. I stopped digging for a moment and sighed; I wasn't sure I had the energy for such a thing right now. Maybe I could just plan on fantastic "welcome back" sex.

"Fuck," I heard Soren swear, with an unusual softness in his voice.

I looked at Billy in question. "He's got a kid." His normally smiling face was downturned and heavy.

I had seen other reapers get them and was glad it hadn't happened to me yet. Babies never even made it to us: their spirits just went straight back to the source, whatever that may be. It was rare, but sometimes we got toddlers. There seemed to be some sort of cut off point of when they were too big to go to the source, but still so tiny.

I could only imagine how hard it was for Soren to dig up a child when he missed his own kids so much. Being a gravedigger I had buried my share of little caskets, and it was those times I had cried while I worked. There was something that felt so unnatural about putting a child in the ground, even though they were the most fragile of all life.

Billy and I stopped working and walked over to Soren. The little boy was dressed in navy slacks, and a comfy but new plaid flannel shirt. His wavy golden hair was fixed just so, and his little cheeks were still chubby with baby fat. He couldn't have been older than three at the very most. I thought of the parents left behind to grieve him and my heart ached.

Soren stared down at the boy, making no movement to wake him.

"I'll do it if you want," I said, and gently touched his arm.

He nodded and stepped out of my way.

I got out my light and knelt down over the boy. I clicked it on, and he blinked.

"Hi there," I said in a gentle voice. "My name is Helena."

"Hi, I'm Robbie." The boy yawned and rubbed his eyes. "Am I in heaven? Are you an angel?" he asked, with now very wide eyes.

"No, sweetie. But I'll try to get you somewhere just as good. OK?" I was relieved he knew he was dead.

He nodded, and I helped him up.

I looked at Billy and Soren. "Where do I take him?"

Soren answered, "There's a place for kids on the other side of the city; it's a big white building. You can't miss it."

I leaned into Soren, "Would I get in trouble if I stopped long enough to get him some ice cream?"

Soren smiled, and my heart melted. "I think that

would be fine."

The child's soft voice broke through the stillness, "Where are we going?"

I leaned down on his level. "A special place just for kids like you. But first, we need ice cream."

His little eyes grew wide, and he grinned from ear to ear, "Are you sure this isn't heaven?"

I looked up to see three vampires making their way to me from across the fields, "Oh, yes," I answered. "I'm sure."

I glanced at Billy and Soren, who had already noticed my friends.

"We'll take him," said Soren.

"You don't mind?" I asked.

"It's fine," Billy agreed.

"You're not comin'?" Robbie's little voice asked with a hint of disappointment.

"My friends are going on a long trip and I need to tell them 'bye. Soren and Billy will take great care of you though. I promise. It was very nice to meet you, Robbie," I told him.

"It was nice to meet you too," he said.

I patted him on the head and saw Soren take the little boy's tiny hand in his as they walked away. I had never been sure I wanted kids, but something about seeing Robbie walking hand in hand with the tall, strong, badass Soren made my maternal instincts flare. In that moment I was glad I was already dead.

The vampires had stopped a short ways away, I assumed to let the reapers leave without frightening the little boy. I made my way over to them, and Grace grabbed me and hugged me.

"Thank you for being there for me earlier," she said,

and squeezed me.

When she released me, I leaned back and looked her over. Her eyes still seemed too wide, but not as animalistic, as far as I could read in their amber depths. She looked much older than her teenage years, but her skin hadn't seemed to age. She was beautiful, and vampirism looked good on her.

"You look lovely," I told her.

"I feel amazing." She grinned, and I glimpsed fangs.

"How did your first feeding go?" I asked.

"It went well!" she laughed. "There was a guy passed out in an alley. He never knew I was even there."

"She's a natural," Andreas exclaimed, with obvious paternal pride.

I smiled and nodded. That sounded like the equivalent of getting your dinner out of a dumpster, but to each their own.

Andreas doted on his new creation, and Grace reveled in her new... life. Boude had been quiet and was standing to the side.

I walked over to him and wrapped my arms around his neck. "You're ready to leave?"

"We are," he said, and placed his hands on the sides of my waist.

"Where will you, I mean, these bodies be?" I asked, lightly tapping him on the back.

"We'll all be at Andreas's in one of the beds. To sleep here is to be awake there," he answered.

"And if anything happens to you there?"

"If we die there, we cease to exist here," he said.

"Are you still sure Rasputin is worth this much trouble?" I asked.

Boude kissed me on the forehead. "It's something

I've ignored for far too long," he said.

Rising up on the balls of my feet, I kissed him on the lips, slowly and softly, but with enough passion to show him he would be missed. I tangled my fingers in his soft red curls—my favorite thing to do. I broke the kiss and smiled at him. He was so lovely, and for a vampire, I supposed he was a decent man. I knew I could never love him, but I liked him a lot. Maybe in this world, that could be enough.

He gave me a smile that could stop a train. "Oh, when I get back..." He winked.

I walked from him back to Andreas and Grace. I could tell from the look of excitement in Grace's eyes there would be no way to talk her out of going. I hugged her again, saying, "Please be careful. You are my best friend."

"I will, Hel. I love you." Grace squeezed my hand in hers.

"I love you too. All of you, take care of each other and come back to me soon," I said.

Together they walked back the way they came, and I was once more left alone in the fields with the dead. So, I started digging.

All the people I reaped in the next passing hours disappeared the moment the light touched their eyes, and I was grateful I didn't have to talk to anyone.

I worried for my friends on their journey, no matter how capable they were of taking care of themselves. From previous conversations with Boude I knew time passed more quickly in the living world.

After a while, I grew tired of digging. I went in to my place and took a hot shower, letting the water beat on my neck and shoulders, even where it stung the bite Rasputin had left me.

I wondered about healing times in this world, and tried to make a note to ask someone.

I got out of the shower and found a silky nightgown Grace had left here. It was too short for my personal taste, but it covered what needed to be covered. I went over to my bed and collapsed onto my new, fluffy duvet.

I ran my arms up and down, feeling the coziness, and rubbed my feet against the softness. It felt amazing. Finally, I grabbed my pillow and just sank into the stillness and wonderful feeling. I hadn't been resting long when I heard someone walking up.

Knock, knock came from my door.

Oh, hell, I whined to myself. "Come in," I called. I was not getting out of bed. What were they going to do, murder me? I chuckled.

The knob turned slowly. It was Soren. He looked around the room for me, and laughed when he saw me stretched out in my bed.

I motioned him over. "Come feel—it's new."

He walked over and petted my fuzzy bed like a cat. "Hey, that does feel nice," he said.

I patted the bed. "Sit."

He did.

"How did the drop off go?" I asked.

"Kids are always a lot of paperwork. But it went fine, and we all had ice cream." Soren rubbed the back of his neck like it was tense. "He was a good kid though, and they'll make sure he's taken care of." He was reassuring himself as much as me.

I smiled, and pulled my hand out from beneath the covers to put on his knee. I knew what I was feeling. There was something between Soren and me: it was potential. He was strong and stable, sexy and dependable—maybe even a little dangerous. No, he wasn't my dark, mysterious Raphael that I loved. And though Boude was a friend and lover, it would never grow into more than that because the feelings just weren't there.

Soren looked down at my hand on his leg with no readable expression. I wondered if he felt any trace of what I was feeling. Well, I was about to make things a lot better, or a lot worse.

I looked up into his steel eyes, and traced circles on his leg with my fingertips. Then I ran soft lines up his leg over his brown cargo pants, and dug my nails in lightly on the way back down.

As he watched me, an intense look came over his face; then he closed his eyes and sighed, giving me the go ahead to continue.

I thought of unbuttoning his pants and continuing my fingers' exploration, but I wanted his lips on mine. So, I sat up in the bed and looked at his face. He was sexy, in a Viking kind of way; or in modern-day-terms, a blonde lumberjack or ex-military way. His shoulders were broad, and his body was thick, but not fat; he was strong and solid… and he was shaking.

I could feel his hands trembling as he brought them around to my back. The feel of his fingers on my bare skin made a chill run across it, and suddenly I was shaking too.

Still not close enough, I came up on my knees in the bed and moved towards him, leaned in, and pressed my lips to his.

The kiss had only a moment of tenderness before the

frenzy that ensued. His tongue explored my mouth and his hands played in my wet hair, pulling until I cried out against his kiss.

He pulled back, "I'm sorry, I can get a little rough. I'll back off."

I had never had anyone be rough with me like that; it was a little hard to admit, but my body was giving me all the signs that we liked it.

"No," I answered trying to catch my breath. "If you get too rough, I'll stop you."

He stared into my eyes with a ferocity I had never seen; it made my heart race. His hand on the back of my head held me there for a moment while he searched my face for any sign that I wasn't being honest with him. Then his fingers tightened in my hair again, pulling just to the point where I winced and closed my eyes. His lips found mine again, and he kissed me so hard I thought that he would bruise my lips.

His mouth fed at mine, and his hands eventually left my hair to explore my body. He would gently run his fingers over the silk of the nightgown, then squeeze my ass or leg. The rougher he got, the harder I kissed him, the harder I pressed my body against his letting him know how much I wanted all of him.

He teased me forever with kisses and touch. I tugged at his pants. "Take these off," I begged.

He laughed and stood up to undress while I watched. My body ached at the sight of him, I couldn't wait to feel him, warm and naked against me.

When he got back in bed, this time he got under the covers with me so that there was only the smallest bit of silky fabric separating us. He ran his hand over my ass and then slipped his fingers between my legs, causing me to cry out.

"Oh God," he said at feeling how turned on I was.

Nervously, I grinned and kissed him, wiggling against him and throwing my leg over his waist.

His eyes were closed, but he shook his head. "It has been a very, very long time since I have been with a woman. I will not let this be over any time soon," he growled, and threw me on my back.

His hands and mouth worked my body tirelessly, and I was weak and trembling before we finally got to the main act.

He wasn't as large as Raphael, but when he slid inside me, I didn't feel like anything was lacking. The weight of his solid body on top of me, and inside of me, I felt like I was being held by a warm piece of iron. My fingers dug into his arms, barely making dents in the skin for the muscles being so large. This was protection; this was being made love to by a warrior. This was being fucked by a barbarian. I loved it.

He knew when and where to be gentle, and which areas could take a little more roughness. I writhed and moaned beneath him, moving away instinctively when he would sometimes pull or bite just a little too hard. Whenever I would pull away, he would nuzzle and kiss my neck so lightly and gently that I would wrap myself back around him tighter… then the whole thing would start over again. Waves of pleasure and pain tossed me back and forth for what seemed like hours. I couldn't count how many times I came, and I knew my legs would not work after this, but God help me, I wasn't about to stop him.

I had been in every position he put me in, and whenever I had tried to take a break and give him some personal attention, he would stop me.

"I just want to enjoy your body tonight, lovely Helena. I'm so glad that you don't mind my more forceful side," he whispered against my breasts, before taking one in his mouth and biting.

I gasped. "Just as long as the forceful is mixed with the sensual," I said in a breathy tone.

With that he swirled his tongue around my nipple, and my whole body relaxed back against him.

"I should let you rest," he said. "We both have digging that needs to be done."

I really wanted to rest, but I felt like I had been greedy. "You haven't finished," I said, looking at his body, that was obviously still ready for more action.

He kissed my lips, long and sweet. "I only finish if it's love. This was wonderful, though."

I was a bit pissed at his statement. I mean, I didn't think I loved Soren yet, but it didn't seem right to say it that way. Plus, it made me feel a little dirty that I'd had nearly a dozen orgasms, and he wouldn't let himself even have one, since he didn't love me. I pushed my pettiness aside and tried to think of what I knew about Soren. He was a devoted family man before his death, a hunter filled with pride and honor.

"You don't want to betray your wife?" I asked.

"It probably seems silly, coming from someone of your culture." He rubbed his beard.

"I think it's very sweet," I said, and kissed him on the cheek.

"I'll get out of here so you can rest." He moved to get up.

I put my hand on his arm. "Soren, would you stay and just hold me while I rest?"

He thought about it longer than I expected him to, but eventually he laid back down beside me and pulled me into his arms. His wide, muscular body enveloped me, and for the first time since I died, I slept.

CHAPTER THIRTEEN

When I woke up, Soren was gone, and I was all right with that. I recalled dreams of Ray and digging with him in our cemetery. The dreams left me longing for those days once more: for him, for home.

I was thankful I didn't dream of Raphael, and I was more thankful there were no nightmares.

As I finally dragged myself to a standing position, the room spun, and my lower body was not too keen on moving after all of my previous activities. I smiled, recalling Soren's fierce attentions.

I wondered how things would be between us now. I hoped it wouldn't be awkward; I really wanted to do it again. Truth be told, I really wanted him to be more than a friend with really great benefits—although, with his devotion to his wife I wasn't sure if I could make that happen.

Walking to the sink took some effort; I was dehydrated and in need of food. I couldn't recall eating more than a bite or two of anything since I had gotten here. Sex really takes it out of you, even when you're dead.

Please let Grace have left something here, I muttered to

myself as I looked in the few kitchen cupboards.

I sighed in relief when I found a box of cereal bars with oats and chocolate chips—then I ate all five that were in the box. Maybe weight gain wasn't a problem here.

Once I felt alive again, pun intended, I decided another shower was definitely in order. Yes, I was just planning to go out and dig, but I didn't want to smell like Soren and sex all day; that could be distracting.

I piled my wet hair into a bun, and put on the jeans I had deemed my "work" pants after Grace had made me pick up several new outfits. A blue t-shirt and boots completed my uniform, and outside I went.

My tools felt a little heavy in my arms, and I knew that I probably would not be digging for too long this time around.

I was just getting ready to start when I heard laughter behind me. I turned to see Soren's face lit up, laughing deep and loud at something Billy had said. I could see by the expression on Billy's face that he wasn't used to seeing Soren this happy. It was a look of, "This is great!" mixed with, "This is weird."

They made it over to me, and I was laughing with them even though I hadn't heard the joke.

"Good morning, Ms. Hel," Soren said in a cheerful voice, and smiled at me in a way that reminded me of all the things he had done to my body recently.

I felt my face redden and quickly looked down. "Good morning, Soren," I smiled, barely glancing up at him—feeling that any upward glance would immediately spill our secret to Billy.

We all worked and talked. For the first time, we all ended up swapping happy stories from our lives: tales of school days—well at least for Billy and me.

Soren told stories of learning to fight, hunt and build things in the village where he grew up. He was as smart as anyone I had ever met; the lack of modern schooling certainly hadn't hurt him.

We laughed at one another's stories, and tried to keep the rare joyous mood flowing. Whenever a painful memory would arise, and our faces would fall or our laughter turned to silence, the other ones would go into another funny anecdote until we were all laughing again.

After countless stories had been heard, and many souls had been reaped, my own body was reminding me I had been a little hard on it.

I ached in multiple places, some of which took some thought as to why and how;and my throat was still sore in the spot that Rasputin had bitten me.

"How does healing work here?" I asked while rubbing my achy neck and shoulders.

"Depends on the injuries: most things begin to repair within an hour. Injuries that would have been life threatening can take the equivalent of a few weeks," Soren said.

"Just like the living though, protein can help you heal," Billy said.

I sighed. "Geez, I need a freaking rule book for this place." I rolled my eyes.

"Time doesn't work the same, but you can get by pretending that it does. There's no day or night, and sleep is optional. Food is optional too, but sometimes it helps to eat. You can get hurt, but you can't die. If you're hurt badly enough, you might wish you could die again, but in time you'll heal," Soren explained.

"Yeah, I've learned most of that," I said, and something hit my mind to ask. "If Rasputin had torn my throat out, I mean massive blood loss or windpipe crushed, what would have happened to me?"

"Blood loss, you would have been weak and in a dreamlike state until you could heal, with the right care. If your windpipe was torn out, you would have gasped for air until it grew back, or a replacement could have been put in," Billy answered, in a way that said he knew more about this than I probably wanted to know.

"So, I would have suffocated until it was fixed?" I put my hand to my throat, thankful to be breathing, even if it was only an illusion.

"Yeah, we don't really need to breathe here. But it's easiest for us to accept things here if we go by living human rules... Something about the way the mind works," Billy shrugged.

Hearing such well thought out musings come out of the backwoods-looking, string-bean-like Billy, was endearing and made me miss my mountains.

"Well all of that sounds horrific," I said.

Billy nodded in agreement. "I've seen a man get his throat torn out. It didn't look like a good time."

"So what's hurting you that you're wanting to heal? Did you stub your toe or something?" Soren asked with a sneaky smile.

I forced my own grin off my face. "My neck, remember? I was mauled by a vampire." I pointed.

He nodded as he recalled the memory.

"I suppose I could use some protein. I've barely eaten since I got here," I said. "Does anyone want to join me?"

"I could go for a steak," Soren said.

I knew I looked as confused as I felt. "There's meat here? That seems wrong somehow. Do they slaughter already dead animals? That's not fair."

Billy laughed at me to the point of leaning over to catch his breath, and Soren just leaned over his shovel with his head down in exasperation.

Soren raised his head and shook it. "No, Hel, everything is simply created here, just like the food we pick up. There's no gardening here, no big farms—unless you want to count this one."

"So somebody just makes it, like magic?" I asked.

"I don't know what's considered magic, but yeah it's just made here. There's a big factory on the east side of the city," Soren answered.

"Ok, let's go get a steak." I picked up my things and motioned for them to follow me.

"All right," Soren said, and picked up his things as well.

"Are you coming, Billy?" I called to him.

"Nah, I'm not hungry and I'm behind on my work. Have fun though." He smiled his gap-tooth smile and waved at us.

I knew how much Billy worked, and there was no way he was behind. I wondered if he knew about Soren and me, either from watching us together, or if Soren just had to tell someone. I wasn't mad or judging; I could hardly wait until Grace was home so I could tell her.

"Ok, if you're sure then," I said.

"Yep, things are all good here," he said.

Soren and I walked to the shed and put our tools away.

"Are we getting cleaned up first, or going like we are?" Soren asked.

I thought about the effort it would take to put on makeup and try to match an outfit. I wrinkled my nose. "How nice is the restaurant?"

"There's more than one. We can go to the casual one." He smiled.

"That sounds great," I sighed.

"Are you really that worn out?" he smirked, seeming quite proud of himself.

"Shut up." I narrowed my eyes at him.

"I guess having dessert is off the menu." He said it so softly I barely heard him.

I was tired, but suddenly seemed to get a second wind. "Hey, I heard food can do magical things. I might be all better."

He smiled at me, and I was so thankful this didn't feel awkward.

We made small talk as we walked through the city. Normally, I barely received more than a passing glance from people on the streets. Walking with Soren, people noticed, and most of them crossed the street to walk on the other side. Some cut down alleys as soon as they saw us, others ducked their heads and tried to give us a wide path.

"Why are people afraid of us?" I asked Soren.

"This is why I don't like coming into the city," he said. "I probably reaped most of these people. It's not exactly a happy memory for them."

I thought about it… Were dead people still as weird about death as living ones?

"You reaped me. I'm not afraid of you." I elbowed him as we walked.

He gave me a quick glance and grin, then he took my hand in his. My heart fluttered for the first time since Raphael.

I squeezed his hand, and was proud to walk right along beside him.

I was a little sad when we arrived at the restaurant because he let go of my hand. But he opened the door for me, which I thought was nice.

The inside of the place looked like any other restaurant that would have the words "roadhouse" or "sirloin" in the title.

No menus, just a server who asked us what we wanted to eat and drink, and trotted off to the back.

Steak with broccoli and a baked potato was what we both wanted, and we both ordered beer to go with it. I still didn't feel particularly hungry, I was just glad to know food would help me heal.

Soren smiled. "You're still over thinking the eating and sleeping thing. Don't. Just pretend like you're still alive, and do the things you'd normally do. You'll be happier for it."

"Yeah, you're probably right," I shrugged, and sipped my beer. It was fine, nothing spectacular. I wondered if the beer was better in heaven or Valhalla, or wherever.

Soren downed half his beer in only a few gulps, then he set the glass down firmly on the table while he made an "Ahhh" sound. He focused his steel gray eyes on me and asked, "So, do we need to discuss what happened last night, or are we good?"

I was so glad he was the one to bring up the issue, but it was still an awkward thing to talk about. "Well, I don't feel weird around you, if that's what you're worried about."

He nodded and waited for me to say more.

"I'd like to know if this is a very casual thing that might happen again, or if there might be some potential for feelings… You know, just to get everything out in the open." I took a drink of my beer because I felt like I needed to be doing something with this nervous energy.

"You're the only woman I've been with since I got here," he admitted. His eyes were fixed on mine.

To me, that meant this could be a serious thing, but I didn't like to interpret things in my own way just because that's how it made sense in my head. So, I just asked, "So does that mean you have feelings for me?"

Soren leaned back in his chair and looked me over with such scrutiny I had to look away. He was gruff but handsome. Now that I knew just how much those eyes had seen of me, and how his calloused hands felt on my skin, I was suddenly *more* self conscious, rather than less.

"Look at me," he growled.

I did, and a good kind of fear gripped my stomach.

"You are strong, and beautiful. We would be good partners." The corner of his mouth lifted in a smile that made his eyes sparkle.

"I appreciate the compliments, Soren. Really, it means a lot." I smiled back, and let that sink in for a second, before continuing, "But I don't want to be with you because we seem to be a good fit. I want to be with you because you care for me, because you want me—or even just for sex is OK, if you only desire me like that. I just need to know where we stand." I was proud of myself for speaking what was on my mind, and I sat a little straighter.

His fingers played along the rim of his beer glass. It was his turn to look away. "It is hard for me to admit feelings for another woman, since my wife."

"I understand that, and I would never want to take those memories from you. But don't you think she's moved on? Wouldn't she want you to be happy?" I let the sincerity in my voice come through loud and clear.

"She remarried, and yes, she would want happiness for me. But one day we will be reunited. I keep hoping one day, I'll look down and it will be her soul that I see."

"How long have you been waiting?" I asked.

"About one hundred mortal years," he answered.

I didn't try to hide the shock on my face. "Soren, there's no way she's still alive."

He nodded. "I'm well aware of that." There was a hint of anger in his voice.

"Where do you think she is? Haven't you worked off your time by now?"

"Yes, a couple of times over. I don't know where she is: I haven't reaped her, and no one else can say for certain if they did. I'm afraid to move on; if I choose a different path than she did, we might never meet again. There's a possibility her soul hasn't been reaped, and she's waiting, and that is what I cling to." His face was stern.

Soren was a bit more broken than I had realized. As much as I loved Raphael I knew I couldn't spend my time wandering the afterlife, waiting for him to die and return to me. I thought Soren's devotion was endearing, and truly romantic, but logically I could only see the pain it was continuing to cause him.

"My ramblings haven't answered your question," Soren said.

I looked at him to continue, but our steaks arrived; then the server brought out more beer. We didn't talk while we ate. I was hungrier than I had realized, and Soren liked to focus on his food. The food was good, exactly the way I remembered it tasting. If you had told me I had just eaten this meal the previous week, I could have believed it.

"Tasty," I muttered between bites, just to say something.

Soren nodded while he chewed.

When we finished, we stood and stretched and left. I started toward the fields, and Soren stopped me.

"Let's wander around a bit," he said.

I changed my direction and stood beside him, hoping he'd take my hand in his again. He didn't.

We walked but didn't talk. There were fewer people out on the streets now, and I wondered where everyone had gone. Maybe in the city they had a more structured sense of time for food and rest and work—unlike us reaping heathens, who did things whenever we felt like it.

I looked up at the boring buildings, and wished at least the architecture from the Quarter had spread to more of the area. But that would probably mean more vampires, and I wasn't sure that was something we needed.

I saw we were walking towards the fountain. I had avoided it since the day I had looked into it. Nothing until that point had made me feel truly dead. I wondered how often Soren had looked in it to see his wife; I wondered how he felt when he looked and realized she was no longer there, but not with him.

Soren looked at me and I could tell the wall he had worked so hard to build around himself was weakening with me. His eyes were usually so cold, and his face unreadable. I didn't know if he was intentionally letting his guard down with me, or if it was just crumbling on its own.

We looked into the water together, and it was just that: water. The sun wasn't shining in our dreary world, and the fountain was large, and lovely. It was a fountain like you might find in any city square. It wasn't magical right now, people weren't crowded around it, and there were no images of the lives we had left behind. Just water, and the white noise of it rushing and falling back into the pool below, gently spraying our skin and clothes.

Soren finally took my hand again and motioned for us to sit on the edge of the fountain.

"I used to come here every day and spend hours. That way I'd have a good spot if the sun shined through," he said.

I shook my head, remembering my experience. "When I looked, it hurt too much. I know I wasn't a very important person, and that life could go on without me, but it hurt." I swallowed, and a few small tears escaped my eyes. Soren watched me quickly brush them away. I laughed. "I'm sorry. I'm pretty sure you've seen me cry more than any other person you've ever been around."

"In the beginning I thought your tears were a weakness. Now I think they make you stronger. People usually cry when they can't carry on, your tears seem to renew your courage." His tone was thoughtful.

Yes. I kissed him.

The time from the moment I kissed Soren in front of the fountain until we made it back to my place was a hurried, albeit horny, blur. There was no taking our time tonight, just a frenzy of passion and skin. It was hard to say it was even better than the previous night, but with that amount of need and desire pulsing through us… it was pretty damn fantastic.

We laid there panting, recovering. I looked over at Soren, sparkling with sweat and flushed from the activity. I kissed his shoulder and licked his sweat from my lips. He raised an eyebrow and laughed at me. He rolled onto his side and pulled me against him, his member pressed into my leg.

"Ugh," I groaned. "You're still ready to go."

"Does it really bother you?" he asked.

"Well, yeah. Girls like to know their lover had a good time as much as the reverse."

Soren stroked his beard and seemed to contemplate this.

I added to my thought, "I mean, I get it, about your wife. But it just feels… unflattering."

He squeezed me tight with my face against his chest, and kissed my forehead. "I do not mean to insult you in any way, sweet Hel. You are perfection in my bed."

So help me, I grinned so big I almost giggled. "Thank you."

"It will take me some time to get used to being with another woman," he said, still squeezing me. "Can you give me that time?"

"Well, I certainly don't want to stop having sex with you now that I know how amazing you are." I kissed his chest and snuggled against him. So big, so warm.

"Good," he sighed as he stroked my hair.

Once again, I slept—this time, dreamlessly.

I woke up feeling better than the previous time I had woken. The food really helped. I smiled, remembering my talk with Soren and spending the night in his arms. I was even happier when I rolled over to find him still beside me in the bed.

His eyes lingered on me with a soft gaze. "Did you sleep well?"

I yawned and stretched. "I did. Did you sleep at all?"

"No, but I didn't want to leave you. Some here have nightmares when they sleep, and I couldn't bear the thought of you being alone and scared." He smiled.

"So you just held me and watched me for hours?" I asked. This was sweet, not creepy—at least that's what I kept telling myself.

"Is that OK?" He furrowed his brow, afraid he had done something wrong.

"I'm not used to people watching me sleep. As long as you were comfortable, I guess it's fine," I said.

"Lying here with you, watching over you, I felt needed. It was a better use of my time than sitting in my place alone, or out digging with Billy," he said, and touched my face.

I intertwined my fingers with his and brought his hand to my lips. "I'm very glad to have you here," I said, kissing the tips of his fingers.

"Now that you are up, we should work!" he exclaimed, and nearly jumped out of bed, leaving me startled and slightly annoyed.

I sighed. "OK, see you out there." I started to ask him if he had told Billy anything about us, but he was dressed and out the door before I could form the words. Work hard, play hard: that was Soren.

It wasn't long until I made my way outside and chose a spot near Soren to dig. We exchanged a meaningful smile but said nothing.

A few minutes into work, we heard cheerful whistling and saw Billy carrying three cups of coffee in a tray, and a bag of something. He was smiling like the cat that ate the canary.

He beamed at us. "Mornin'. Thought you all might enjoy some coffee and muffins after your long night."

My eyes widened, and when I looked at Soren, he had the same concerned look on his face as well.

"What do you mean, 'our long night,' Billy?" Soren asked, trying to keep his face serious.

Billy chuckled. "You know what I mean: long day, long hours, whatever. Y'all think the walls here are sound proof, or somethin'?"

I turned about fifty shades of red, but couldn't help laughing. Soren gave him a tight lipped smile, but nodded.

"Point taken."

"And I saw the two of you when you got back from the city; holding hands, couldn't stop kissing… You walked right by me." He grinned and set down the coffee and muffins. "I love it," he said shaking his head, and picked up one of the coffee cups.

We laughed, and all smiled at each other. We sat on the ground and enjoyed our food before getting back to work.

It was kind of nice that Billy knew and we didn't have to be so secretive. It made it more real, more stable. I was glad Soren seemed just as happy as me about the issue.

I took a deep breath and realized I was feeling happy. It had been so long since I felt that. Just the thought of the word felt like warmth flowing all over me. I reveled in it, in Soren, in Billy. I was only missing Grace.

I was digging and felt Soren creep up close behind me. He leaned in and whispered in my ear. "Since you gave us up, next time, I'm going to stuff a gag in your mouth."

I made a face and offended sound in protest, but couldn't stop the smile that followed. Well great. I was still coming to terms with this masochistic side Soren brought out in me, and now the last thing I wanted to do was work. *Torture.* That was probably what he was going for.

I worked several hours, then went into town to stock up on groceries.

After combing the aisles, I had a cart full of protein and caffeine, along with a coffee pot that I desperately needed. *That should fuel work and sex for the next few days.* I had a few extra plates and mugs that Grace had brought in, but picked up a few pots and skillets to cook in. *That should be enough to feed myself.*

As I was walking back through town I saw the dark, regal entrance to the Vampire Quarter. I wondered how my friends' journey was going. I estimated they had been gone a couple of weeks, in living time, and had questioned why they couldn't come back to me while they slept there during the day—something I could ask when they came back; if they came back.

Once back at my place, I put the food away and washed the new cookware. The advice I had been given was right: the more I tried to follow rules like I was living, the easier my day felt. If nothing else, it was just an activity to keep me busy. And now that I was with Soren, I didn't feel the need to burn every second of every hour by digging. I felt almost normal, and smiled to myself in my contentment. I wasn't certain this was what I wanted forever, but for now, I'd take it.

I went back out to dig, since I wasn't tired. Sleep wasn't necessary, but it had seemed to energize me. I hadn't been able to fight it after the exhaustive love making Soren had put me through. But the idea of sleeping here still made me nervous, knowing the nightmares I could have.

I walked out into the gray and brown atmosphere that made up my world, and tried to find some kind of beauty in the bleakness. I failed, and sighed, and used my boot to shove the shovel into the soft earth. Billy and Soren were nowhere to be seen, and even though there were other reapers, they seemed to always be on a schedule that was different from us. I wondered if Soren had scared them away, like he tried to do to me when I first came. I smiled at the fact I was the only female reaper, and had won him over so well.

"Hel," I heard Soren's voice behind me.

I wiped the sweat from my brow and turned to see him and Billy walking towards me.

"Hey," I smiled sweetly, not hiding the fact I was happy to see him. My smile faded when I saw how serious his face looked.

"What's wrong?" I asked.

"They're back. We just saw Andreas in town," Soren said.

"What did he say?" I asked.

"Nothing, he didn't see us. We just saw him in the store. He was picking up some makeup," Billy said.

Questions flooded my mind: Why wouldn't they come see me first? How long had they been back? Were they avoiding me because something bad had happened?

"I need to get over there," I said, and handed my shovel to Soren. "Please finish this plot?" I leaned in and kissed him on the cheek without even thinking twice.

"Let me go with you," he pleaded. "You don't know what you're walking into."

"No, I think it's better if I go alone. I promise I'll be careful, and I'll come back as soon as I can." My eyes searched his for understanding. This wasn't the time I needed him to be all super macho and powerful.

He pushed his chin forward and straightened his back. It was a wound to his pride not to protect me, but he respected me and let me go.

I held myself to a fast walk as I made my way through the field. It took more energy to hold myself back than it did to run, so I ran. I ran all the way to the city's edge, where the brown of the dirt stopped and turned to gray cement.

To my surprise, my lungs didn't burn with the effort, and my side didn't feel like a knife had been jabbed into it. Maybe once things settled down I would consider taking up running.

The entrance to the Quarter was as beautiful as it

was intimidating, but I didn't stop to think about it; I simply went on inside.

I didn't run, only because it was difficult to recall where the apartment was, and I was afraid I'd walk right by it.

Black streets, black buildings, tight alleyways and soaring sky lines—so beautiful, and so menacing.

I saw the little stoop that looked like the one Boude and I had been on. I was more certain than not that this was Andreas's apartment. I quickly ascended the steps and used the elaborate door knocker that confirmed my suspicion.

Andreas opened the door. His eyes were unreadable, but he didn't speak to me. Instead he called over his shoulder, "It is her. Should I let her in?"

Boude's voice sounded strained and stressed. "Yes, yes, of course she can come in."

As I stepped in I thought about telling Andreas that he needed better door manners, but what I saw quickly made that seem insignificant.

Boude was on the red velvet couch, leaned forward with his head in his hands, looking anything but relaxed. Beside him in one of the matching chairs sat a man that seemed more familiar than he should have. He was dressed in black, his beard was long and thin, and his eyes were endless pools of blackness.

Who else would be here? The realization hit me like a punch to the stomach. "*Rasputin,*" I whispered, and stepped back in shock. He looked just like the picture I had seen in my school books while growing up. Boude might not have been certain of his origin, but I was convinced this was the same guy.

He stood and reached for my hand. There was no

way I was letting any part of my body that close to him. I stepped back and unconsciously put my hand on my now healed neck, where he'd once sunk his fangs.

His smile told me he was glad he frightened me. "Helena, correct?" he asked in a thick accent.

I nodded.

"I am sorry, I do not remember what happened during those years I was starving, but I was told I recently attacked you. Thankfully, my friends here finally saw fit to rescue me."

The way he said 'finally', I wasn't sure if he was truly grateful, or simply pissed they had waited so long. I ignored the man, who was creeping me out even worse now, as himself, than he did as a starving, decaying vampire who wanted to drain me.

I looked at Boude, and backed even farther away from Rasputin. "Where is Grace?" I demanded.

Boude raised his head from his hands and sighed. I almost screamed at him to answer me, when I heard her voice.

"I'm here Hel," Grace called from the doorway behind me.

I was so relieved I almost cried. I turned around to run to her, but I froze..

When I saw her, my universe stopped. One side of Grace's face was as lovely as it had ever been, showing her brilliant amber vampire eye. But the other side her face was raw, clawed, and one of her eyes was gone—completely gone—only a gory, red ruin of what was once there.

CHAPTER FOURTEEN

I GASPED AND COVERED MY MOUTH. IT WAS awful, and I couldn't pretend like it wasn't.

"I'm OK, Hel. It doesn't even hurt anymore," Grace said, touching one of the long gashes that traced the front of her left cheek.

I went to her and put my hands on her shoulders. "Who did this to you?" I asked, choking back tears of desperation and rage.

"I'm afraid, that was my mistake." The evil dark haired man spoke from the corner.

I turned to look at him, and if my eyes could have set him on fire, I would have roasted a marshmallow while he burned.

"What do you mean?" I asked through gritted teeth.

"When Andreas and Boude released me, I was starving and practically feral. Grace was so recently turned that she didn't smell like a regular vampire to me. I thought they had brought me food," he shrugged. "I felt terrible once they tore me away from her and explained the situation. I was happy to have only caused a little damage."

I lunged for him—I would tear his throat out with

my fingernails and teeth if I had to.

Hands on my arms and shoulders stopped me just short of my reach. Rasputin was still seated, looking completely undisturbed.

Grace and Boude had my arms.

"You call this 'a little damage?'" I screamed at him, flicking a gesture at Grace's bloody face, while my upper arms were still held pinned.

"It was only an eye. It could have easily been her throat, and there would have been no coming back from that." The gleam I saw in his beady eyes let me know that his statement was as much of a threat as anything.

"Vampires heal extremely well, right?" I asked. "Isn't that one of the perks?" I needed something to hope for.

Everyone was too quiet, but Andreas finally stepped out from the doorway in the kitchen area.

"In the mortal world, wounds can be harder to heal, and if that damage is inflicted by another vampire, especially at her young age… It is likely permanent." He was leaned against the wall furthest away from me.

I turned my head to look at Boude, hoping my eyes showed the desperation I was feeling. "You promised you would watch out for her."

He broke eye contact and dropped his head, but never loosened the grip on my arm. "I know I have failed you as a friend," he said.

"In more ways than one," Andreas said almost inaudibly.

Boude and Grace both shot Andreas sharp looks. The blonde vampire in the doorway shrugged.

"Why not just get it all in the open? I see no use in saving these secrets for another time." He smiled, enjoying the bit of trouble he was causing.

My body sagged in their grip. More bad news? "Just tell me," I conceded.

"Let me this time," Grace said to Boude, and I saw a slight nod of his head.

"While we were traveling together, we needed to share a sleeping space. We didn't want to travel back here everyday because we needed to conserve our energy. It started innocently enough, but the cold, the darkness, and my new bloodlust ran deeper than…" she paused, looking away.

"…Deeper than blood." I finished for her, realizing the direction this had taken. "The two of you slept together," I said as I tried to process this news.

"She was a teenager when she was died. Isn't there a rule against that or something? Vampiric statutory rape?" I was sickened and confused. I shook them off of me and backed away from everyone so I could catch my breath.

Rasputin sat in his chair with a smug look of contentment on his face. I wanted to wipe it off with a sledgehammer.

"I was only eighteen when I died. So you see, it's not as big of an age difference as you claim," Boude said.

I almost argued that he had died who knew how many centuries before Grace, but realized that argument would hold no weight if and when they learned about Soren and me. Dammit, I felt protective of Grace, and Boude had been my lover… err, friend with benefits. My head spun with internal dialogue of feelings and logic, neither of which supported the other. I felt my friend had been maimed, and was now being taken advantage of by the people who were supposed to care for her.

"I need to get out of here," I said. Everything in the room looked blurry, and the air felt thick and heavy. I tried to avoid looking at Rasputin, who was the one clear, still image my eyes tried to rest on.

Grace touched my arm as I tried to make my way to the door. "Please don't be angry with me. Stay, lets talk," she pleaded.

I turned to her. "Grace, I love you and I'm glad you made it back. And I'm more sorry than I can say that you were hurt. I just need some time." I made my face soft and squeezed her hand.

Her face showed the disappointment she felt, but she let me go. A tear ran from her one lovely crystalline eye down her unmarked cheek.

I was drunk when I finally made it back to the fields. Feeling pissed off at everyone, I decided digging would be a good way to release some anger.

I had my shovel in one hand, and the bottle of gin I had been nursing in the other. I set the bottle down in the dirt and started digging. My shovel didn't slide into the dirt as easily as it normally did, and nothing seemed to cooperate.

"Dammit!" I yelled at my shovel and the ground. Some hair had escaped my messy bun, and I brushed it back with my arm. Ok, try again.

I kept spilling the dirt from my shovel back into the same spot I had just gotten it from, over and over.

My hands tightened on the shovel and I bit my lip. I brought my foot up to kick the shovel down into the dirt and missed, scraping the length of my calf down the edge of the shovel.

"Son of a bitch!" I yelled in pain, and beat the shovel against the ground while continuing to scream.

My shovel was quickly pulled from my grasp. Enraged, I turned to see Soren holding it, with a very concerned look on his face.

I glared at him. "Give it back."

"What is the matter with you?" he asked, looking at me like I had two heads.

Pouting, I sat down on the ground and took a swig from my bottle. "I'm not in the mood to talk about it."

"Are you finished throwing your tantrum?" he asked.

Being referred to in such a childish manner rekindled my anger, and I looked at him with rage in my eyes. "No," I said.

Soren sighed. He dropped my shovel and walked over to me, and through a series of movements my inebriated self couldn't follow, somehow scooped me up and threw me over his shoulder.

"What the hell are you doing?!" I yelled, pointlessly beating against his back and trying to kick my legs, but he had too good of a grip on them.

He opened the door to my place and set me down once we were inside.

I had to blink several times and place my hand on the wall to keep from falling down. "I'm not in the mood for sex, and I don't want to calm down. You might as well go home." I stood facing him with my hands on my hips.

"You're a danger to yourself. I'm not leaving you," he said without even raising his voice.

I walked over to him and shoved him. "You're not my protector."

Soren leaned towards me and swung the door behind me shut. His face was serious and his gray eyes turned cold. He stood straight and looked at me as he stepped forward, causing me to back up. My back hit the door, and he put his hand around my throat, squeezing, but not to the point of pain. My hands found his shoulders and tried to push him back.

"I will decide what you need me to be, and when you need me to be it," he said, with his face only inches from mine.

I tried to swallow but couldn't. "Fuck you," I gasped.

He softened his grip, and I pushed him away again. His hands pinned mine against the door.

"Look, I know you're pissed. You're mad at the vamps because they did whatever vampires do, you're mad at me for telling you they would do that, and you're mad at yourself for getting dragged into their bullshit. You've searched for every reason to hate this place, and then you made some peace with it. Now things are rocky and you're pissed off again. It's fine: hate it, hate them, hate me—just get it out of your system so you can move the fuck on." His voice resonated, like he was speaking to an army preparing for battle. His eyes were kind, and staring right into mine.

I blinked at him and wriggled my wrists until he let go. Dammit, I did not want him to be right; the anger felt good and solid. I wanted to keep it and feel it, to touch it and hold onto it—it gave me a drive and purpose. I could keep feeding anger and it would grow. The anger could make me strong. I flexed my fists and wrists with the thought.

As if he read my mind, Soren said, "Show me, show me how mad you are. Take it out on me. Let me see what this anger is doing to you."

Immediately, I hesitated. I could hurt him—at least, I could try. But I knew I cared about him, and no matter how angry I was, I knew I could not bring myself to cause intentional harm to someone I cared for.

I slipped from between the door and Soren's body, just out of reach, and shook my head no. I wrapped my arms around myself and dug my nails into the skin I could touch, to ground myself.

Soren walked over to me and took my hands, laying them down on his forearms. "Use me," he said. "Dig your nails into me, mark me with the pain you feel. I can take it... and I'll enjoy it."

I searched his face and found no trace of anything but wanting. I laid my nails against his skin and dragged them down the length of his inner arms.

Soren shivered and closed his eyes. I hadn't drawn blood, but the scratches were obvious and would leave welts for several hours.

"I can take harder," he breathed.

I stepped in against his body, and kissed him, a soft touch of lips. I could feel through the thick material of his pants, he was enjoying this. I tugged at his shirt and helped him take it off. I ran my hands up and down his back and chest and pressed my body against the warmth of him.

I kissed his lips and neck and chest, and as his breathing became more labored, I dug my nails into his shoulders and scratched as far as I could manage. The strained sound he made was a good incentive to do it again, this time down his chest.

I looked at all the little red lines I had made on his body, and couldn't help but smile at my artwork. Soren had offered to take my pain: to let me hurt him, so I would hurt less. The pain I needed to let out so desperately was the pleasure he was seeking. It was the same for me the night I was pinned beneath him, at his mercy. We needed each other, needed each other's pain.

I kissed him again, this time, with happiness. "Thank you," I whispered in his ear while I ran my nails lightly down his spine.

His hands came up to play in my hair before suddenly pulling a handful hard enough to make me catch my breath.

"My pleasure." He scooped me up and carried me to the bed.

CHAPTER FIFTEEN

A SOFT KNOCK AT MY DOOR WOKE ME UP. I yawned and stretched and touched the side of the bed where Soren had been before he left me.

I smiled, recalling his goodbye kiss after we made love, and how when I asked him to stay he told me I had "been too bad." I knew that actually he had made plans with Billy to check the fields for any areas that hadn't been attended to lately. I had been drifting in and out of sleep since he had gone.

The knock came again, this time a little louder. I stood up, wrapping my furry blanket around myself, and went to the door. I opened it, and was only a little surprised to see Grace.

She stood in front of me in her leather jacket over a black t-shirt, and a yellow punk-rock plaid mini skirt with black ankle boots. An eye patch that matched her skirt was covering the hole where her eye once was, and makeup lessened the severity of the remaining scars that trailed down her face. Her lips were dark red, and in her hands she held a box of chocolate cookies.

"Come in," I said.

"Hel, I uh…" Grace tried to get the words out, but was fighting back tears.

I shook my head at her. "I'm not mad anymore." I went to her and hugged her.

"I'm not your mom, and Boude and I had no claim on each other. All I care about is that you are OK and happy."

She smiled and sniffed, wiping away a few tears, regaining her composure. "Going to get Rasputin was scary and hard—the hardest thing I've ever done." She nodded as she remembered. "But I made it. I lost an eye, but I survived," she proudly beamed. "Boude looked out for me, and never treated me like a child. He showed me what I'm capable of, and he believed in me. We're happy." She smiled, biting her lip, letting a tiny glimpse of fang show. "And I don't regret getting turned at all."

I hugged her. "I'm proud of you. Still a little scared, but so proud."

We pulled back from our hug and both wiped a few tears away.

"Lets have cookies," I said, "…after I find some clothes."

Grace eyed me with an arched brow while I changed. "Why were you naked? You never sleep naked."

I grinned. "I'll tell you about that while we eat cookies." I paused. "Can you eat cookies or have coffee?"

Grace laughed. "I can, I can eat whatever I want. I only have to have living blood to survive."

"Great! Can you put on some coffee?" I asked, not really wanting to hear about my friend's new hunting skills.

"Sure," she laughed.

We spent hours talking and laughing. Grace told me about the trip to get Rasputin, and the more I learned about the dangers they encountered, the more thankful I was to have been ignorant. Now that I had met the true Rasputin and not just the shell, I honestly wasn't sure which one was more dangerous—or even if that rescue mission had been a good idea. I, however, was not a vampire, and therefore didn't get a say in the matter.

I filled Grace in on my new relationship with Soren.

"For real?" she shrieked.

"For real," I said.

"You've kissed Soren?" she asked.

"Oh, honey, we've done a lot more than that," I told, her and felt my face heat up.

She gasped. "Serious Soren…" Grace mused. "Well, give me details."

I told her as much as I could, right until he left my bed this morning. When I finally stopped gushing, Grace said, "You are absolutely glowing. He seems really great for you."

She smiled and flashed fangs at me. I knew she hadn't gotten the hang of hiding them yet. Grace sipped her coffee and tugged at her eye patch.

She saw me watching her.

"The damn thing itches," she said.

"It doesn't hurt?" I asked.

"No, not anymore. The pain was pretty indescribable when it happened, but Boude made sure I fed quickly, and it healed—as much as it could heal, anyway." Her silky black hair swung in front of the eye patch, covering half of it. I knew she had changed the direction of her natural part when she brushed her hair to help cover it.

"It hasn't hurt how you see yourself, I hope," I added.

She sighed. "Well I don't love looking at the gaping hole where my cool new eyeball was, and the red scratches that will always look fresh aren't super attractive. Makeup hides those pretty well, and the eye patch makes me look kinda badass, so I'm embracing my new look."

I smiled and agreed. "Between the eye patch and the fangs, you definitely look like someone not to be fucked with."

Grace smiled proudly.

"Has Boude been good through everything?" I asked.

"I couldn't have made it without him," Grace answered. "Andreas is great fun, but he's a city guy. He was as lost as I was out in the cold mountains. And since the incident, Boude kisses both sides of my face every day, and tells me how strong and beautiful I am."

"I really am happy for you," I said, and I meant it—mostly.

"Death is a million times better than life," Grace giggled.

I smiled at her, so happy it had worked out that way for her. I wish it had been the case for me. I was learning to enjoy this new "life," but I missed my home, my mountains, and still a huge part of me missed Raphael.

It was good, though; I was letting go and learning the ropes of the afterlife. I had a good boyfriend, I had a job that was still helping people, and I had at least a few friends. I would be thankful.

We chatted a while longer and made plans to meet up at least once a week to catch up and fill each other in on the goings on. I helped her pack up her things from while she lived with me, and hugged her goodbye, and missed her as I watched her go. The house wasn't the same without her living here, but at least I could invite Soren over whenever I wanted.

I was washing the cups Grace and I had used when I heard my door open again. I turned to see Soren peeking around the door.

"Everything in here OK?" he asked cautiously.

I laughed and motioned him inside. "Everything is fine."

"Good. I saw Grace leaving, and I think she was wearing an eye patch. I was afraid that might have been your doing, or that she drained you, or that you were just really upset again. Although, if you don't mind me saying so, that worked out really well for me last night," he smirked.

Seeing Soren smile was one of my favorite things to witness. It was like seeing a rare white buffalo, or a unicorn. When I was the reason for those smiles, it felt even more special.

"Last night worked out pretty well for both of us," I added.

"So the two of you made up?" he asked regarding Grace.

"We did."

"Do I ever get to find out the whole story of what happened?" He walked over to the bar and sat down.

"Will you come over tonight? I can tell you

everything then. Fair warning though, I might get upset and need to be calmed down." It was my turn to give him a sly smile.

He looked at me like I wasn't to be trusted, but then he pulled me in close when I walked over to him. Wrapping my arms around his solid body always gave me a thrill. I felt so small and delicate when he wrapped his arms around me.

"What are you getting into now?" Soren asked me.

"I think I'm going to head into town and get a few things. When I get back, I'm going to work." I kept my face neutral, but was secretly excited about picking up some new lingerie to wear tonight to surprise him.

"Sounds good. I'll be in the fields." He kissed me on the cheek and gave me a smack on the rear. "See you later."

I was alone once again. I stepped into the bathroom and looked in the mirror. I looked exactly the same as I did the day I died.

My hair was still the same length, still the same shade of dirty blonde, and my eyes were still clear. I felt as though I should look older from all the things I had been through, but no, I'd look like this until whatever I moved onto next.

I made a note to pick up some makeup, and maybe a curling iron. There was no point in wearing the sexy lingerie if the rest of me still looked like a Plain Jane.

At the lingerie store, I picked up a black lace bra that tied up the back in a corset style. I tried it on in the store because I was worried about getting it home and not being able to get it tied by myself. Luckily, the laces were stretchy, and it wasn't as complicated as I had feared. A pair of matching black lace boy-shorts completed the look, and even I had to smile at my reflection in the mirror. I knew it would look even better with my hair down, clean, and curled.

I picked up some makeup and a curling iron next, and a small bottle of perfume that smelled like jasmine flowers. On my way home, I stopped in the coffee shop to have a cup of tea.

I chose a table in the back corner where I could watch people if I wanted, or put my head down and tune everyone out. I was doing the latter when I heard my name.

"Ms. Helena," the smooth voice spoke.

"Hello, Boudewijn," I said before my eyes even fell on him. Oh but how they fell on him. His fiery hair shimmered as it fell around him in waves, his emerald eyes deep, and still disconcerting.

"May I?" He waved his hand at a chair and I nodded.

"Thank you." He sat down. "Grace told me she came to see you this morning. She said things were better between you?" He made the last words a question.

"Yes. We're fine," I said. I knew what question was coming next, but I hadn't decided how I felt about it.

"How are we?" He pointed his finger back and forth between us. "I would hate to think I've lost my friend."

"Boude, I'm not happy with you. You didn't exactly keep your promise to keep Grace safe, and there is still a part of me that believes you are taking advantage of her naivety." I didn't sugar coat my thoughts. He was older than me by hundreds of years: he could handle the truth.

He nodded. "Yes, I can see how you would feel that way." He paused, then reached for my hand. I let him place his cold hand on mine, and looked at it like a bug I was thinking of swatting away. "And if I hurt you emotionally by being with Grace, it was never my intent. I truly believed you and I were only physical," he cooed.

I pulled my hand from beneath his and held it in front of his face to stop him. "That was not my issue with the relationship between you and Grace." I had a whole list of other reasons just dying to make their way from my brain to my mouth, but I resisted. How much good would it really do? It would change nothing.

I finished my tea in one long sip, and stood up to gather my shopping bags and leave. I looked at Boude, who was still sitting. "Despite my reservations, I wish nothing but the best for you and Grace. You are both my friends, and all I want is her happiness." I leaned in. "So if you hurt her, I will stake you, hide you where no one will ever find you, and leave you to rot for all of eternity."

Boude's eyes widened. "Understood." The word was soft.

"Oh, and keep Rasputin far away from me," I added, and left.

I put my things away and tidied around the house when I got home. I had picked up two coffee and vanilla scented candles on the shelf at the coffee shop, and I placed them near, but not too close to the bed.

I grinned as I laid out my lingerie and new girly things to show off tonight. I was grateful Soren was open to the idea of a true relationship, but it bothered me that he still hadn't truly let himself go with me. I was hoping my efforts tonight, along with how compatible we seemed to be, would help him cross that boundary soon.

I went outside and gathered my tools, making my way a good distance out into the field. The sky was gray and dull, but just for a moment I closed my eyes and imagined being back home in my mountains. I pretended to feel the softness of the grass underfoot, and a light breeze blowing across my face. I stared into the evening sun as it went down, painting the sky with reds and golds and violets. I smiled at the memory of so many sunsets I took for granted, then opened my eyes and sighed.

Soren and Billy were digging a few rows away, and I waved as I chose a spot behind them. As usual, I ignored the marker and began shoveling the earth away to free whatever soul was awaiting the next chapter.

Before too long I had the body unearthed, and grabbed my flashlight to awaken the soul. I crouched down over the body, and for the first time, really looked at it.

I looked up at Soren, and back down at the body in front of me. I looked back and forth between them for a long time, trying to figure out what I was feeling, and what I should do.

Soren caught me looking at him and winked at me, his way of letting me know he was excited for tonight. I mustered up a smile for him, and thought about him: the man I could fall in love with; then I looked at the body before me and thought about *him*: the one I already loved.

There, right before my eyes, was the man I had missed every day that I had been dead… Raphael.

THE STORY WILL CONTINUE IN

DIGGING UP THE DEAD

ABOUT THE AUTHOR

WILLIE E. DALTON is the author of *Three Witches in a Small Town, The Dark Side of the Woods,* and *The Girl Who Digs Graves* (Book 1 of the Gravedigger series). Willie is a full time writer at her home in the Appalachian Mountains of southwest Virginia. When she isn't writing, Willie spends most of her time volunteering with the local cat rescue group.

Find her online at:
WWW.AUTHORWILLIEDALTON.COM

www.ingramcontent.com/pod-product-compliance
Lightning Source LLC
Chambersburg PA
CBHW032020050726
47590CB00006B/2246